Catherine's terror escalated when fingers wrapped around her ankle…

She tried to scream, crawl, kick, but her body wasn't working right.

From deep in her stupor, she realized it must be Porter Stone. Her father's killer was trying to draw her free from under the car. She tried to yank away, but she couldn't fight off the effects of the explosion. From inside a thick cloud, she felt Stone tugging at her arm. With the heavy dog on one side and Garrett's body blocking his access, he only succeeded in moving her a few inches. Catherine wanted to resist, to call out for help, but her mouth refused, her brain slow and sluggish.

Garrett hadn't moved. Was he unconscious? Worse? Her pulse skittered.

The tugging continued. Now Stone had snagged a fistful of her jacket. Inexorably, he was sliding her away from Pinkerton and Garrett.

Despair clawed at the edges of Catherine's mind. Her father was dead. Her sister, gone. And now Stone would have her, too…

Dana Mentink is a nationally bestselling author. She has been honored to win two Carol Awards, a HOLT Medallion and an RT Reviewers' Choice Best Book Award. She's authored more than thirty novels to date for Love Inspired Suspense and Harlequin Heartwarming. Dana loves feedback from her readers. Contact her at danamentink.com.

Visit the Author Profile page at LoveInspired.com for more titles.

Fugitive Search

DANA MENTINK

LOVE INSPIRED SUSPENSE
INSPIRATIONAL ROMANCE

LOVE INSPIRED SUSPENSE
INSPIRATIONAL ROMANCE

ISBN-13: 978-1-335-98008-3

Fugitive Search

Copyright © 2024 by Dana Mentink

Recycling programs
for this product may
not exist in your area.

For questions and comments about the quality of this book, please contact us
at CustomerService@Harlequin.com.

® is a trademark of Harlequin Enterprises ULC.

Love Inspired
22 Adelaide St. West, 41st Floor
Toronto, Ontario M5H 4E3, Canada
www.LoveInspired.com

Printed in U.S.A.

But the very hairs of your head are all numbered.
—*Matthew* 10:30

To my sisters, the very best pack a gal could ask for.

ONE

Was everyone watching her?

No, they weren't and even if they were, they'd see only a nondescript woman known as Molly Hartman sitting in a run-of-the-mill car in the cramped coffee shop parking lot. An unmemorable name for a woman easily forgotten. Hopefully.

She pulled her hat down low on her brow as she shut off the engine. The man in the feed truck next to her gave her a nod, which made her shrink in the driver's seat. Friendly, she told herself. That was all. A small-town phenomenon absent in bustling San Francisco, precisely the reason she'd rented an apartment there. The best way to be anonymous was in a crowd.

And the woman seated inside the shop who glanced out the window in her direction was likely lost in her own thoughts rather than paying much attention to Molly's arrival. She popped a tiny mint, her mouth dry as ashes. There were a thousand residents in Whisper Valley, the most northern of California towns. Not like they never had visitors, especially since they boasted a new luxurious inn and even a classic car showroom.

So why did she feel like an exotic zoo animal, drawing everyone's attention?

You know why.

She wondered for the millionth time if that moment ten years ago, when she was barely seventeen, would define the rest of her life. Her fingers clenched into fists. New start. New chapter. But her boldness quavered and a chill swept her body. She wasn't fully ready to embrace her unexpected freedom completely, even after the arrest of Porter Stone, the man who'd murdered her father. Stone was finally in custody, after she'd spent a torturous decade looking over her shoulder.

He escaped before. He can do it again.

She shook off the thought, but the prickly feeling on the back of her neck remained. Possibly it always would, the damage from an invisible wound that would never fully heal.

She'd lined out a series of baby steps, wobbly lurches toward the life she intended to reclaim. The meeting at the coffee shop was the first one, though it did make her nervous to return to Whisper Valley, so close to where she and her sister had grown up. But a chance to visit Uncle Orson could not be overlooked. If she snagged some work too, that'd be a bonus.

She'd chat with Beth Wolfe and nail down the job designing her marketing materials. In truth there was no need for a face-to-face; she'd stressed that again and again to the boss of Security Hounds Investigations. The website she'd pored over had a plethora of photos of the beautiful bloodhounds they used in their casework. There was absolutely no reason for her to have coffee with Beth instead of meeting via Zoom. Molly could cull tons of gorgeous images for the ads from the online shots. If they ever decided to include photos of the human staff, that'd be simple to arrange as well. At the moment there were no people pictured on the Security Hounds website. Smart, she figured, for an agency that probably rubbed elbows with criminals. She had no headshot on her own website either, for different reasons.

"I never work with anyone I don't eyeball in person," Beth Wolfe had cheerfully insisted.

At least the woman had acquiesced to meet at a coffee shop instead of her ranch. Molly had met another Wolfe long ago. Probably no relation and she doubted he was still around after a decade, but she didn't want to take a chance of encountering anyone from her past.

She smoothed her ponytail, got out, and pushed through the coffee shop door. The crowded space was everything she'd hoped for. Bustling. Noisy. She scurried inside and slid into a booth in a far corner just as her phone buzzed.

See Uncle O yet?

She pictured her younger sister Antonia's elfin features, a more delicate version of her own. Zero patience, that girl. With a smile she replied. Later. After my meeting. Can't wait. It was still surreal that within the space of two hours she would be able to hug Uncle Orson again without the necessity of a clandestine meeting. After ten long years…

Her sister replied. Stepping back into our old lives feels weird.

Her fingers flew as she answered. I know, right? See you soon, Tony.

Not soon enough.

"Coffee?"

Molly jumped at the waitress's arrival, dropping her phone with a clatter and hurrying to snatch it up again. The waitress quirked an eyebrow.

"Maybe you've had enough caffeine already." The smile took the sting out of the comment.

She shrugged. "I'm meeting someone here. Beth Wolfe."

"Ah, okay. I'll bring two coffees then. Beth likes hers black. You?"

"Black is fine." Molly pulled the glasses out of her bag and put them on, wishing she'd done it sooner. They were clear glass, no prescription, but the sleek frames were a comforting shield between her and the world. *Still disguised, Molly? No need for that anymore, is there?* Why did she cling to these crutches—a fake name, accessories? Justice had been a long time coming, but Stone was no longer a free man. She removed the glasses and shoved them into her purse.

The waitress returned with two mugs filled with hot brew. She'd taken a sip when someone slid into the booth next to her, placing a sleek navy folder on the tabletop.

A man with dark hair and irises the color of walnut, a man who looked painfully, heart-lurchingly familiar.

"Morning," he said.

She jerked and knocked over her coffee.

"I got it." He immediately grabbed napkins from the empty booth next to them and slapped them down to contain the flow. "I've been spending time with my nephew. You develop sharp babysitting reflexes, let me tell you."

"I—I was expecting Beth Wolfe."

He looked up from the soggy napkins, chagrined. "Oh, man. My apologies. I'm Garrett Wolfe, Beth's son. She sent me in her place."

Beth's son? Her head spun. Unbelievable as it was, Garrett Wolfe sat before her, in the flesh. His genial smile, the easy way he carried his six-foot frame, the confident jut of his chin. The past flashed to the present and she pictured him as she'd seen him a decade before, an impossibly handsome twenty-one-year-old in a blazer and slacks, a badge clipped to his belt. Detective Garrett Wolfe. She felt like screaming at her own stupidity. Of course, he was Beth's family. She'd been too eager for the job and her homecoming with her sister and uncle to think it through. He looked the same except for some lines around his mouth and the crow's feet that deepened as he regarded her. Words piled up on her tongue, refusing to exit.

"Mom sends her apologies. She asked me to cover the meeting because she's prepping for back surgery and the doctor wanted to see her at the last minute." He walked to the coffee station, appropriated a pot and a clean mug as if he owned the place, and refilled hers.

Settling in again, he took the mug that had been poured for his mother, added a slug of cream and two sugars before he took a sip. "Perfect," he said before offering her the cream.

"No, thank you." Her pulse was in high gear. Garrett Wolfe, the detective who had been assigned to her father's murder case, obviously didn't recognize her. Not surprising since she'd been a teen back then. How should she go about handling the conversation? Or bolting for the door? Bolting definitely held more appeal.

Her brain buzzed helplessly as Garrett chatted on. "You know it's funny. I thought I knew you at first when I rolled in, but I can't dig up the name *Molly Hartman* from the old memory banks."

That's because he hadn't known her as Molly Hartman. It was flooding back in icy waves. Garrett had been acquainted with Porter Stone before he turned killer, never completely believed he'd been guilty even though the arrest warrant was issued. She remembered a long-ago conversation—she, Uncle Orson, her sister, all drinking bad coffee, huddled together in the police station chairs Garrett had settled them into.

"They won't find Porter guilty," her sister had hissed in her ear. "He has too many friends in this town, cops included."

Her words had proven true, but not in the way they'd imagined. Porter Stone, genial tow truck driver and part-time pizza delivery guy from a longtime local family, had escaped Garrett Wolfe's custody at the arraignment and remained at large for ten years until his recent arrest. A stew of emotions bubbled inside her.

Garrett had stopped talking and was gazing at her with mild puzzlement.

"So you're a private eye?" she blurted.

He blinked at her abruptness. "Sure am. I haven't yet purchased a trench coat and fedora, but I've been working for Security Hounds since I left police work."

Left. Confirmation that he was no longer a cop. How nice for him that he could simply walk away and into another career. Did that make their meeting better or worse? She didn't know.

Her phone pulsed with a text but she left it in her pocket. Why had she assumed he'd moved away? Did it matter? It sure felt like it did.

He was still regarding her in that way that made her stomach flip. "You sure we haven't met? I'd like to say I never forget a face, but honestly, I'd lose track of my head if it wasn't attached at the neck, says my sister Stephanie."

She doubted that. His smoky eyes, halfway between brown and amber, sparkled with intelligence and something else. Suspicion? She sat up straighter. What did she have to feel uncomfortable about? He was the one who hadn't believed Stone was guilty and forced her to live under a secret identity for the past decade. Her phone vibrated again. She ignored it, a flood of anger rising.

"All of a sudden I'm not feeling very well." Truth. Her gut was heaving and her entire body was freezing cold. "I'll arrange with Beth to reschedule." She got up from the booth, ignoring his surprise.

He scooted out and stood. "Did I say something to upset you?"

"No, like I said, not feeling well. Tell your mother I'll be in touch."

She dropped a few dollars on the table and practically ran out, heedless of the phone twitching in her pocket. In a flash she was behind the wheel of her car, cranking the ignition. She had no doubt she would regret her hasty departure but she was compelled by a desperate need to escape.

He'd followed her to the diner door, one hand holding it open as he stood there in confusion.

The phone buzzed yet again before she'd put the car in Reverse. She yanked out her cell and checked the screen. Her sister. Two words.

He's escaped.

And then a shadow loomed from the back seat, hot breath bathed her neck, a blade pricked her throat.

"Drive," a voice said.

Even before she found him in the rearview mirror, she knew.

Garrett wasn't a cop anymore, but his instincts were clawing like the bloodhounds at the shrubs he was perpetually replacing. He returned and collected the folder Molly had left, added a few more bucks to the pile to make it worthwhile for the waitress and hustled to the parking lot.

He got a glimpse of brunette hair through the windshield

of Molly's car as she headed to the parking lot exit. Her shoulders were hunched as if she was attempting to make herself smaller. Mentally he replayed the conversation, trying to land on something he'd said that might have offended her. Nothing stood out to him, but it wouldn't, would it?

She'd left. Her prerogative. A woman could change her mind and Molly clearly had after meeting him. Was that what was bothering him? His ego taking a blow because she obviously didn't like him? He'd armored himself with charm his whole life and he felt rattled by her rejection as he got into his vehicle. That had to be it. His problem, not hers.

Pinkerton greeted him with a throaty woof through the open window of the car in its shady parking place. "Hiya, Pinky." He slid in and started his vehicle. The bloodhound's red coat shimmered in the morning sunlight as he scooted as close as his cable-and-tether system would allow, his wide nose quivering, digesting all the clinging scents from Garrett's foray into the coffee shop.

"In answer to your question, it didn't go well, and I don't know why," he said to his dog. Her car had reached the edge of the lot, ready to turn onto the main street. Without thinking, he goosed the gas and took up position a cautious distance behind her. Pinkerton licked the back of his seat. The dog had a strange tendency to slurp pretty much anything.

"I don't know why I'm going this way either. Might as well take the scenic route back to the ranch, right?"

Pinkerton flapped his fleshy lips. Agreement—had to be, or the dog knew Garrett was fixed on his senseless mission. Pinkerton was spectacularly good at trailing and he loved training lessons as much as he did licking cushions, but nothing topped riding in the car for Pinky, so he wouldn't mind the detour.

And why are you following her exactly? Instinct. The kind

he used to have as a cop. The kind that was screeching in his ear that something was wrong. Then again, he might still be rationalizing. *Not a cop, Garrett, and for good reason.*

His phone beckoned him. It would only take a moment to call the ranch, talk to his mother, his twin sister, Stephanie, but what would he say? He'd upset their potential marketing hire and he was following her because he had an odd feeling? Ridiculous, they'd tell him, and they'd be right.

Just take one more look. See if you can figure out why she seems so familiar at least. Maybe then he wouldn't be awake all night thinking about it.

He pushed his speed, sidling up next to her at the light. If she flashed him a look of pure irritation, that would be enough to send him packing, tail between his legs. He bent his head to peer through his passenger window at her. She turned to him, lips tight and face pale. Her mouth opened as if she might say something, then she jerked her attention back toward the front window, staring straight ahead with a clenched jaw.

Odd reaction. Wasn't it?

He craned to see into her back seat.

Was that…? A shadow? A blur? Nothing at all?

Though the light was still red, she took off.

She was rolling away, out of reach, out of his life. Should he let her go?

Once upon a time he'd been sure of himself and who he was, confident that he was doing what God made him to do. But ever since his last murder case as a detective, it was as though he'd been transported back to those dark days of insecurity.

"I think she's in trouble," he said aloud. He looked at Pinkerton in the rearview, the saggy eyes steady and reassuring.

If he was wrong, he could turn around, pretend it never happened, keep it to himself. No one would ever be the wiser.

But if he was right...

In the distance she turned onto Silver Creek, a road that would parallel the river for a while, a wild stretch that funneled into a narrow wooden bridge not suitable for cars. One way in and one way out unless you were on foot. It was a popular path for hikers and horse riders.

Why would Molly go that way if she wasn't feeling well? His mom had told him the woman lived in San Francisco, so she might be visiting someone in town, or staying at one of Whisper Valley's two hotels, rather than making the eight-hour drive in one day. But there were no houses in this direction, no cabins.

Her car would be out of visual range soon. When he stopped at another light, he pulled the binoculars from the glove box and risked another quick look.

Was that a shadow in the back seat?

Movement or his eyes tricking him?

The seconds ticked by, matching the thudding of his heart.

Any working instincts left, Garrett?

Or your imagination running wild?

She turned off the main road.

He made his decision, tossed the binoculars and drove after her.

TWO

Molly battled tears from the moment she'd left Garrett's car behind. She'd not sent her silent plea for help clearly enough for him to pick up on it when he'd approached. He'd probably thought she was being snooty, especially after she'd practically run from him at the coffee shop. It might be the last mistake she ever made, not telling Garrett Wolfe the truth.

Porter Stone imprisoned her with one arm looped around the driver's headrest, long fingernails digging into her chin. In the other hand was the knife, still pressed to her throat. The skin under her jaw stung where the blade had bitten. A shallow cut, but if he exerted a little more pressure…

Ten years before her brain would have denied what she was experiencing. This couldn't be happening, didn't happen to normal everyday people. But all those years ago, Stone upended her happy life with the suddenness of a devastating earthquake. When he murdered her father, he'd taught her a terrible lesson—everything could be stripped away in a moment.

She forced a question through her quivering lips. "You were arrested. How'd you escape?"

"Oh, I'm real good at that. You should know, right?"

"Where are we going?"

"To a private spot where we can get some things straight."

Somehow, she kept her shaking leg on the gas pedal as they drove the softly winding road to a graveled turnoff. Should she try to wreck the car? Leap out? But when she slowed, he upped the pressure of the knife against her windpipe. The slightest movement on her part and he'd bury the blade in her throat. He was a killer, that much he'd already proven.

More tears pricked her eyes but she blinked them back. No time for that. She needed her wits about her because she was certain of only one thing: he would not get whatever he desired of her. Period.

"What do you want?" Her voice was high, unrecognizable even to herself.

"I'll tell you when it suits me." His breath smelled of cigarettes. "What's the matter? Anxious? Doesn't feel good to be on the run, does it? Any idea the kind of dives I've lived in for the past ten years? But I'm not going to jail and I'm not running anymore. I'm done."

Not running and not going to jail. What choice did that leave?

The terror was dizzying.

She knew what was about to unfold. She'd taken the self-defense classes that stressed over and over never to allow yourself to be taken to a secondary location, especially an isolated one. But the road had grown steep, the drop-off into the trees such that she doubted she would survive if she managed to drive them off the road.

What do I do?

She could think of nothing. Yet. The route he demanded took them to a spot she'd visited as a teen when they'd come to town to see Uncle Orson, a quiet, serene stretch of tree-studded ground where a small bridge crossed a mountain fed river. It was gushing now, from the recent rain, loud and rumbling. The ground was soggy and it was a cool and cloudy spring day, not attractive for hikers. All those facts made it a perfect spot to kill someone without risking witnesses.

You're not dead yet.

"Stop here," he commanded.

She rolled onto a rutted patch of wet ground. One moment was all she needed. She'd leap out and run. The quick view in her mirror gave her the impression that Stone was stocky and didn't look to be in great shape. She had abject terror, a flood of adrenaline and arduous gym workouts to fuel her speed.

He kicked open the rear passenger door, and while he was climbing free, she saw her chance.

She flung herself out. *The trees. Make for the trees and hide.*

But he must have anticipated that because he swept out a foot and caught her ankle. She crashed on hands and knees to the ground, rocks flaying her palms.

"Get up," he snapped.

Knees protesting, she stood. *Keep watching. Another chance will come.* It had to. They were parked on a narrow ribbon of ground that tumbled away on one side with a mountain butted up to the road on the other. Ahead was the slender wooden pedestrian bridge, reminding her that her daredevil sister had walked the railing like it was a tightrope in their growing-up years when they'd visited their uncle.

Would someone come along in spite of the weather?

A committed hiker or fisherman who could help?

She darted a look at her captor. Stone was surprisingly clean-shaven for a fugitive, wearing too-tight clothes that hugged his ample waist, hair cut close to the scalp. How had he escaped custody?

He moved closer, blocking any escape route. She scanned for an opportunity to kick out, but he kept his body angled away. She tried to rub off the feel of his hand on her wind-pipe. All he had to do was squeeze or slash. No one would hear. They'd find her body at some point, too late to help. Her throat throbbed from the slight cut he'd given her at the light, along with the order to drive on. He didn't deserve to have power over her, or anyone, ever again. She tried to formulate another plan.

He interrupted her train of thought with a question. "Where is she?"

"Who?"

"Antonia," he sneered, "your darling sister. Where is she?"

Molly swallowed. There was no way she would give up her sister no matter what he did. "Why do you want to know? So you can kill her too? Dad wasn't enough?"

His nostrils flared. "I *loved* Antonia. She was supposed to be my girl."

She gaped. "After you killed our father? She should be in a relationship with a murderer who destroyed our family?"

Quick as a serpent, he darted a hand into her pocket and pulled out the phone, backing her against the car so he could keep the knife at her throat while he snaked a look at it. "Unlock it."

Sweat beaded his forehead. He looked young, always had that boyish face, but the mischievous eyes were flat now, filled with hatred, the skin pouched and puckered under-neath. One of his front teeth was chipped. He'd been living hard. Well, so had she and her family. What had she ever done to Stone? What had Antonia or her father done?

She glared at him. "You're so smart, unlock it yourself."

"Do it," he shouted, the knife dancing on her skin. An-other trickle of warmth told her he wasn't bluffing. With trembling fingers she keyed in the code. Her texts were all deleted, a practice she'd scrupulously maintained. Except the most recent string from Antonia. The last one said it all.

He's escaped.

Stone laughed when he read it, awkwardly tapped a text with one hand and sent it.

He darted a look toward the narrow road. The knife blade moved back a fraction from her throat. "Took me so long to figure it out."

"Figure out what?"

His red-rimmed eyes narrowed. "I ask the questions."

"The cops are looking for you, aren't they? They'll catch you. You'd better run. Right now."

He grimaced. "Oh, no. I'm not going anywhere until I get back *everything* I lost."

Everything. Including her sister. Stone had always been infatuated with Antonia. The feeling wasn't mutual, which had fueled his rage, she had no doubt.

Anger flamed inside her. "You're not taking anything else from my family." Then she slammed his arm aside with her wrist and kicked out with all her strength. She'd aimed for his knee, but instead connected with his upper thigh. He reeled back, swearing.

She dove for the car. The keys were still in the ignition. One more second and she'd…

He grabbed at her arm and wrenched her away.

She spun, falling onto her back, kicking at him with all her strength. Her heel caught him in the jaw and snapped his head back. Her phone clattered to the ground but she scrambled up, grabbing it as she went. He was getting to his feet, blood streaming from his mouth. He was between her and the car so she turned and ran.

Her mind fired conflicting commands at her. *Get to the bridge. The road. Hide. Call for help.* She made it only a few yards before he grabbed her jacket, jerking her back, twisting. She fell hard, the breath driven from her lungs, rocks grinding against her stomach.

Again she felt the knife, this time poised between her shoulder blades.

Garrett knew Stephanie would get help faster than he could. He'd finished texting her his SOS and freed the weapon from the under-seat lockbox by the time Molly had stepped from her car. As soon as he saw that, he began his stealthy creep toward them using the trees for cover. Pinkerton was in silent mode, surprisingly quiet for a 110-pound animal. Not a protection dog, but his bark was as startling as an air-raid siren. Garrett planned to leverage that fact.

He glimpsed a man through the branches and his heart plummeted. Garrett was still digesting the news he'd gotten five minutes earlier in a call from his cop buddy while he was following Molly. Porter Stone had escaped police custody twenty-four hours prior during a transfer from one jail to another and he'd been spotted near Whisper Valley. A dragnet was in place, community bulletins issued, and it was likely a matter of time before he'd be captured. Mind boggling. Porter was a fugitive once again, an even more desperate one no doubt, and now Garrett was within shouting distance of him. But why had he targeted Molly Hartman? Molly broke away, running, with Stone in pursuit.

"Down, Pink," he whispered.

Pinkerton sank unhappily onto the pine needles.

Stone was crouched over Molly, who'd sprawled stomach first on the ground. Garrett sprinted over the hump of the slope and bellowed his command. "Drop it, Stone."

Stone started so violently at Garrett's arrival that Molly scrambled to her knees, crawling away a few paces. Excellent. Garrett aimed his pistol. Cop rule: never draw a gun unless you're prepared to use lethal force. He was resigned to do exactly that to protect the terrified woman who'd skidded to a stop. Tears formed glistening trails down her dusty cheeks.

"Come over here, Molly," Garrett said evenly. He could see that her legs were trembling. She inched toward him uncertainly.

Stone gripped a knife, close enough to lunge at them both. His nose bled, his lined face almost unrecognizable from the young man Garrett had known a decade before. Back then Stone had been a lover of animals, an avid bowler, able to quote a movie line to fit every occasion. This was not that person, not anymore.

"You're surrounded, Stone." *If surrounded could consist of one ex-cop and a very large dog.* "There's no way out."

Stone looked around, calling his bluff. "Yeah? Don't see any backup."

Garrett eased his gun to one hand and lowered the other to his waist—the signal.

Pinkerton, watching from his perch, saw the cue and began to bark madly. The sound bounced and echoed against the rocks, vibrating in his eardrums.

"See? Second unit and they brought the dogs. No need to make this hard on yourself. Drop your knife and you walk out of here without getting hurt."

Stone stood frozen, his face stark. Garrett had seen the expression before, the one that meant there was nothing left to lose. Was there anything more dangerous than desperation? His stomach dropped, weapon still aimed. "I don't want to hurt you, Porter."

"That right? 'Cuz you're some kind of friend?" He shook

his head. "You said you believed in me, Garrett. Remember? Even at the arraignment you wanted to try and help me."

"I did try and you bolted."

"I was going to jail. That's where you'll put me again, soon as I let go of this knife."

"I'm not here to arrest you. I left the force. Not a cop anymore."

"Oh, I heard. Some fancy detective now. I've been living like a rat all this time while you and the sisters here enjoyed your nice cars and fat bank accounts."

The sisters here...

Molly craned her neck in his direction, posture rigid with fear. The unusual tint of her eyes, the darkest of blues, like the morning shadows on Mt. Shasta.

He got it. Not Molly Hartman.

She was Catherine Hart.

He pictured her sister, Antonia, and their father murdered by Porter Stone. He swallowed. "It's not like that. Let her go and we'll talk about it, you and me, okay?"

"You're an investigator now, big shot. Have been for years? And there's nothing you could have done for me in all that time?"

Garrett's pinprick of guilt widened to a fist. He'd believed in Stone's innocence back in the day. Then he was brought back to earth. Hard. He flicked his head toward Catherine. "You attacked this woman. Must have been tracking her, right? Innocent people don't do that. You proved I was wrong to believe you."

Stone shook his head slowly. "I should've known."

Garrett wasn't going about this correctly. He needed more time for the cops to show. Stall. *Build rapport, don't antagonize.* "I'm sorry. We got off on the wrong foot. Let's start again. Come on, man. We know each other. Your dad and my dad were fishing buddies. You can tell me what's going on here and we can straighten it out. It's not too late."

Stone shook his head. "Yeah, it is. It's too late for anything but laying down the hurt."

He kept his tone calm. "Your dad's a good guy. He wouldn't want…"

"Shut up," Stone snapped, the knuckles around the knife clenched white. "Don't talk about my father."

Garrett was about to switch strategies when there was noise from the other end of the bridge, the cheerful chatter of approaching hikers. Bystanders, oblivious to what they were walking into. A cop's nightmare.

Stone realized his opportunity. He smiled and backed up until he was centered in front of the bridge approach. He knew Garrett couldn't shoot, not without risking injury to the people behind him.

"People on the bridge," Garrett shouted. "Stay where you are."

The hikers did not hear or didn't understand. Two men with bulging backpacks appeared, water bottles in their hands, bewildered at seeing a man with a gun facing another clutching a knife, and a bleeding woman between them.

They stopped a few paces behind Stone.

"What's—" one of them began.

Stone eased sideways and gestured to them with his knife. "Keep going. Slowly."

Hands flung up, they obeyed. Stone kept the hikers between himself and Garrett. Five steps were all Stone needed to draw next to the open driver's side door of Catherine's car. In a flash, he hopped into the driver's seat, started the engine and pulled a squealing U-turn. The hikers scrambled back onto the bridge.

Garrett had only a moment to grab Catherine's arm and

haul her to the trees before the car plowed toward them. The front bumper shaved bark off the trunk of one where they'd sheltered and Garrett spun her deeper into the trees. Stone jerked the wheel and drove away.

"Pinkerton," Garrett called.

The bloodhound churned up in a flurry of flapping ears and scrabbling paws. "Watch," he said.

Pinkerton plopped himself at Catherine's feet. No one would come near her without a canine ruckus.

"It's okay now. Stay here with Pinky for a minute." He took her shaking hand and placed it on Pinkerton's glossy flank. Immediately she began to stroke him. Comfort that only a dog could provide.

He went to meet the hikers, this time with his private investigation ID out and his gun stowed under his shirt.

"Cops are arriving soon." He kept a distance from them since they were obviously still spooked.

"You're one of those bloodhound private eyes, aren't you?" the shorter man asked. "I saw your dogs at the K-9s for Cops show."

And what a show that had been, ending in the kidnapping of his brother Roman's now-wife. "Yes."

"So that guy," he continued. "The one with the knife. Who was he? Why was he after that lady?"

Exactly what he didn't want to attempt to explain.

Pinkerton's bark made him whirl around.

Catherine was lurching away, Pinkerton's ears whipping his face as he confusedly looked between her and Garrett. "Watch" typically meant staying with a stationary person or object. So what was she doing? Garrett had no better idea than the dog.

"You two stay here until the cops arrive." Without waiting for a reply, he ran after her.

She was unsteady in her movements, but still she'd made it down the slope to his car by the time he caught up. He stopped to suck in a breath as she slid behind the wheel, Pinkerton whining and barking when she didn't open the rear door for him.

Hands on hips, Garrett watched her.

She checked the ignition, then yanked down the sun visors. Finally she bent, presumably to search the glove box.

"Catherine."

She swung a look at him, her dark hair coming loose from the elastic.

"You're safe. Police are coming and Security Hounds too. You don't have to run."

Her mouth twitched. "I need the keys."

He arched an eyebrow. "No, you don't."

She smacked a hand on the wheel. "Garrett, I need the keys. I can't explain but I have to go right now."

"You're in shock. You've just suffered a—"

"Now," she commanded.

They stared at each other. This wasn't a trauma-driven reaction. She was scared, but not irrational.

"Tell me," he said simply.

She paused. "You worked on my father's murder case."

"Yes—"

She cut him off. "You never believed Porter Stone was a killer." Her tone was hard as diamond, the accusation clear. "He almost killed me just now so maybe that's enough to finally convince you. If I don't get out of here, he'll kill again. I need the keys."

Her eyes burned holes in him. He'd been wrong about Stone. What had it cost this woman? Her family? He pulled the key ring from his pocket. "Not until you tell me where."

She thrust the phone at him. "Stone sent this text pretending to be me. To my sister."

He leaned close, noting the trembling of her fingers.

The little screen lit up.

It's okay. Just heard the cops got him again. All safe.

And her sister's reply:

What a relief. See you at Uncle O's.

"I've texted, but she isn't replying."

Stone would know the address. Everyone in Whisper Valley and the region beyond did. Orson lived in a beautiful house at the top of a ridge, visible for miles.

He was already texting his sister. "We'll alert the cops. They'll roll a unit to—"

"Garrett." Her tone cut him to the bone. "My father's dead. I've spent a decade living a lie. My sister and uncle are all I have left." She shoved a palm at him. "Keys. Now."

"The police…"

"How did they help me before?"

The question hung there in the air.

She might as well have said, "How did you help me before?"

The system had failed her—he'd failed her. If Stone got to her sister and uncle before the cops did…

"One condition," he said as he moved. "I'm driving."

THREE

Catherine willed her uncle to answer the phone but it simply rang endlessly. She alternately tried her sister's cell and clung to the door handle. Branches whipped the car as they flew along. She didn't need to give Garrett directions. He'd know where her uncle lived. She and her sister had been unable to stay in their family home in nearby Durnsville after the murder, so they'd moved in with Uncle Orson. Garrett had shown up at the mountain house countless times with questions, endless questions, but he'd never answered hers.

Porter Stone killed our father. Why won't you believe us?

Garrett hadn't, not completely. For some reason she couldn't fathom, he'd not been fully convinced of Stone's guilt even after the arrest. Hence his last-minute interview with Stone just before his arraignment. Hence Stone's dramatic escape from custody. Hence her family's decade of terror. If he'd believed her back then, how different things might have been for her and her sister.

Garrett's fingers strangled the wheel, rocks pinging the chassis. When his phone rang, he answered via Bluetooth.

A woman's voice blasted through the speakers. "What do you think you're doing?"

Someone from Security Hounds. Probably his sister, one of the two listed on the website.

Garrett told her their destination. "I've got Molly, er, Catherine Hart with me on this call."

The long beat of silence was telling.

Garrett looked at her. "It's my sister Steph. She works for—"

"I know." Catherine kept her gaze lasered out the front window. *Just get to Uncle Orson and Antonia.* She willed him to go faster but they were already on the edge of safety for the winding road.

"Garrett," Stephanie said, "You need to stop right now and let the police handle this. I just got more details. Stone injured a cop when he escaped. They were moving him to a less crowded facility when he got free and made his way here. Cops will recapture him."

"We have to make sure her uncle is—"

"No, you don't," Stephanie snapped. "They're cops and that's what they train for as you fully well know. Red lights, sirens, Kevlar, the whole bit. You're a—"

"Civilian." A vein jumped in his jaw. "Steph, just roll Security Hounds to the bridge on Silver Creek. See if they can find a scent article to track Stone if it becomes necessary. At least secure the scene until a cop arrives. I'll report in when I can."

"Garrett…" Her voice dripped with warning.

He ended the call.

Catherine knew Garrett probably agreed with his sister, that their mission was pure folly. But Garrett's opinion didn't count. *His* family was still intact and the remainder of hers was hanging by a thread. Once they got to Orson's he could wait outside, follow the rules, do whatever he wanted while she took care of her own.

Garrett yanked a glance at her. "Are you sure you're not hurt? My sister will get an ambulance rolling—"

"I'm okay." But her neck stung and her body ached from diving to the ground. Minor pains compared to what she'd experienced emotionally. The dog in the back snuffled in her ear and licked her, and she reached out to push him away but found herself stroking his massive neck instead.

"Back, Pinkerton," Garrett said. "Sorry. He's the friendliest dog you'll ever meet, but he's a licker."

She regretted the animal's withdrawal as he obediently flopped down on the back seat. She could use a friend.

"Your sister Antonia's a year younger than you, right?"

She nodded. "I've only seen her a handful of times in the last ten years. We've been in hiding."

He frowned. "Threats? From Stone?"

"Yes. We changed our names, moved to different cities, but somehow he found Antonia everywhere she tried to set down roots. Sent her letters and texts. Broke her car window. Threatened to kill her and me too, like he'd killed my father. My uncle helped us start new lives." If you called what they'd been doing living.

Garrett's mouth twitched and she heard him exhale. "I didn't know. After I resigned I was kept out of the loop, officially."

Resigned, probably shamed after Stone escaped his custody before the arraignment. She shifted. Sad, since Garrett had seemed to her to live and breathe the job. For a moment she considered the gravity of wearing a badge. She could commit colossal mistakes in her line of cyber work, nowhere near the stakes for a cop. One slip and a killer went free. The thought subsided again under a pile of anger and resentment. "When I heard from my sister last month that Stone had been arrested, I thought we were finally safe, and now he's managed to escape again."

How did he feel with the weight of guilt that must be bearing down on him? The foot of the sloped road beckoned and Garrett tackled it fast, but not fast enough to suit her.

"My uncle was threatened by Stone too, to divulge our whereabouts. Phone calls from untraceable numbers."

"Any ideas why Stone was so determined to get to you?"

She darted a look at him. "Isn't it obvious? Revenge that our testimony was going to put him away forever. That and he was obsessed with my sister, upset that she didn't want to date him and angry at my father for trying to run him off. He's not going to rest until we're all dead."

He took in what she said, mulling it over, which irritated her more. *What other motive could there be?*

A siren wailed in the distance. "Cops are close."

Fear cinched her nerves tight. What if they were too late?

Around a turn, the black bars of the wrought-iron security gate came into view. Her heart dropped. She could not hold back a whimper. Pinkerton responded with a whine and another lick to her neck. The gates were open, tire tracks showing where a vehicle had rutted the mud. Stone had indeed gotten there ahead of them.

"How did he get in the gate?" she called over the roar of the engine.

Without answering, he stomped on the gas and drove their car through, the landscaped grounds a blur as they roared up the drive. There was another vehicle there with a Protection Services logo on the side. Whose? No sign of her rental car unless it was parked around the back. Perhaps Antonia had arrived in a taxi or Uber?

Please, no. Don't let Antonia have made it here yet.

The front doors were open, one swung wide to reveal the entryway and a sliver of the den, her uncle's favorite room, with the wide windows that framed the purple Cascade Mountains.

The open doors…she could hardly process. Her hand was on the seat-belt buckle before they stopped.

"Stay in the car." Garrett slammed it into Park, engine still going. "Wait for the cops."

He didn't give her time to answer before he was sprinting across the lush grass, a gun he'd pulled from a holster out and ready. He stopped at the entrance, darting a look inside before he vanished into the interior.

Lord, please… But she'd stopped asking God for much the night her father was murdered. Gotten the message loud and clear that He wasn't listening. She was rigid in the seat, the window rolled down, the smell of pine thick in her nostrils.

A woman's scream pierced the air, high, shrill, mingling with Pinkerton's plaintive howl.

Electric shock rippled her body. It came back in a rush, her father lying on the tiled kitchen floor, blood pooling from a head wound, his eyes closed, one hand outstretched as if he was trying to protect his daughters one last time. A scream, so sharp and primal, rang out that night and she'd not realized it was her own. That scream still echoed in her memory and mixed with the one she'd just heard.

Antonia.

Heedless of all logic, good sense and Garrett's command, she leaped from the car and sprinted for the open front door.

Garrett had cleared the den when the woman's scream exploded from upstairs. He swiveled his weapon, trying to both track the corners where any attacks would most likely originate and keep the heavyset woman in his sights. She stood frozen on the top step, her hands raised, palms out; the box she'd been carrying tumbled halfway to the bottom.

"Who are you?" he shouted.

She hadn't gotten out a reply when Catherine sprinted

through the door, stopping so fast her sneakers squeaked on the tile. No way. Another civilian on scene and he still had no idea where Stone might be.

"It's my uncle's housekeeper, Vivian," Catherine said from behind him.

Vivian was shaking. "I was in the attic, packing some things up for your uncle's wife. I heard someone shout. I…"

Garrett's nerves were about to explode. "Come down the stairs and both of you go outside. Right now."

Catherine ignored him. Her face was pale as milk, tears brightening her navy eyes. "Where's Uncle Orson?"

Vivian shook her head. "I don't know. He was in the garage when I got here before I went up to the attic."

"What about my sister?" Her voice broke on the last word.

She shrugged helplessly. "Antonia? I haven't seen her for years. Is she back?"

"Both of you out," he repeated through gritted teeth. "Now. Please."

Vivian obeyed but Catherine was already sprinting to the door that no doubt led to the garage. He wasn't going to convince her to act sensibly, rationally. The best he could do was to try to protect her.

He ran after her and slammed a palm out to shut the door the moment she tugged at the knob.

She turned on him. "Get away from me. I've got to find my uncle and my sister."

He elbowed her behind him. "At least let me go first. If he's behind this door with a knife or gun, we'll both find out soon enough," he snapped.

That made her go still and he was able to maneuver them both to the side. Crouching low, he flung the door open and edged in, once again darting a look immediately to the corners of the room first, then scanning. Sunlight flooded in through the open garage, stinging his eyes. The rental car Catherine had driven was parked cockeyed, the sides scraped and marred, but no sign of Stone, Orson or Antonia. He exhaled and she pushed in behind.

"No one here," he said. The tire tracks on the drive hinted that Stone had appropriated a vehicle from Orson's garage and escaped that way.

His gaze traveled to the tools scattered on the painted cement floor—a wrench, a screwdriver. Hers did too, then her fingers went to her mouth. No way her uncle had left his immaculate garage in such a state unless he'd been forced to.

He could hear entry now, officers pounding through the house. "Stay still for a minute, okay? The cops are coming."

He holstered his weapon and stood with his hands up. Cops poured in—Officer Hagerty, a long-timer he'd worked with on a few Security Hounds cases, and two other younger officers hired after he'd quit the Whisper Valley force.

Hagerty holstered his weapon. "House is clear. Got a guy outside, detained."

"Stone?" Catherine said.

Hagerty narrowed his eyes at her, trying to figure out her involvement in the situation. He'd transferred in as Garrett had resigned so he'd probably only heard snippets. "No. Name's Tom Rudden. Says he was here to meet Orson about repairing the security system."

"Did he see what went down?"

"Says he arrived to find the gate and the door open. Called nine-one-one and waited. Heard a car around back, maybe a shout. Wasn't going to put himself in harm's way. Smart."

The pointed comment was directed at them both. His cheeks flushed. "I had reason to believe her uncle and sister were in immediate danger from Porter Stone." He explained the details.

"Security guy wants to talk to you," one of the officers said to Hagerty.

Hagerty nodded. "How about we all leave this scene so our evidence people can do their jobs?"

They followed him out to the front, where a large, sandy-haired man with a paunch stood in a T-shirt and jeans, the security company logo on his sleeve.

"This is Tom Rudden," Hagerty said, by way of introduction.

Tom nodded, leaning forward eagerly. "I was here to do a repair of the security system for Mr. Hart. Gate was acting up. Bummer, right? Too bad we didn't do it last week, huh?"

Garrett winced at the tasteless remark.

"Did you see my uncle?" Catherine demanded.

"Nah. Just talked to him on the phone. I rolled up and figured I'd better check out the open front door so I parked. Before I got inside I thought I heard a shout. Went around the side yard to check and I hollered to ask if everything was okay, but no one answered so I called nine-one-one. Thought I heard a car leave out the back garage area." His eyes widened. "So what happened? Someone hurt?"

"We're looking into that," Hagerty said smoothly. "Mr. Rudden, you told an officer you saw something that might help?"

"Oh, yeah," he said. "Saw it when I was in the side yard. Didn't touch it, of course, you know, for evidence purposes and all that."

He led them to the fringe of budding rhododendrons that overlapped the lawn. "Caught on these bushes. Saw it glinting. See?" He pointed eagerly to a gleaming band, the kind that women used to gather the hair back from their foreheads. It sparkled with faux jewels that caught the light and sent it dancing in all directions.

He noticed Catherine jerk, as if she'd taken a blow to the middle. He reached for her arm, feeling her tremble.

"What is it?" he said softly.

"That's my sister's," she whispered. "I sent it to her for Christmas."

Garrett shook off his inertia and raced to his car, then turned off the engine and let Pinkerton free. "Got a job for you, Pinky."

He clipped on a long lead and guided Pinkerton over to the hair band Hagerty had photographed and dropped into a plastic bag. Without a word Hagerty gave it to Garrett. He crouched next to Pinkerton and offered him the opened bag.

The dog shoved his head into the bag, snuffling up gulps of air.

"Can he track my sister?" Catherine said.

"He can track anyone." At least until the point they got into an automobile. Even bloodhounds couldn't help much then.

Hagerty bent his head to listen to his radio. "Do you know the make and model of your uncle's car?"

Garrett felt Pinkerton staring at him, wondering why humans were so irritatingly slow.

"He has an SUV—gray," Catherine said. "He told me on the phone when we spoke last that he bought it for his birthday."

Hagerty passed the info along via his radio.

An officer hustled over. "Clear. No one's on the property except the housekeeper. Her husband brought her to work early this morning. Side camera caught someone leaving in an SUV. No visible passenger."

No visible passenger. Orson and Antonia could have been rendered unconscious or bound and put in the trunk.

"We're canvassing now, got an APB out for the car."
Hagerty patted Catherine on the shoulder.

He heard her swallow hard. Her uncle and sister missing.
A nightmare come to life again.

"I'll track with the dog. Antonia might have gotten away,
run into the woods. Orson too, maybe."

Hagerty nodded. "I'll let my people know. Text when you
have something."

"Find," he told Pinkerton firmly.

The dog lurched so mightily Garrett almost lost his footing as they beelined for the woods to the east of the house.
He heard Catherine fall into step behind him. There was no
use telling her to wait with the cops. If it had been any of
his siblings—Stephanie, Kara, Chase, his adopted brother,
Roman—he wouldn't have waited either.

They jogged to keep up, the dog plowing through the tall
grass, speeding several yards, stopping for an abrupt sniff
that almost had Catherine stumbling into Garrett from behind, then another sprint.

He could read the signs, the erect tail swishing in an excited pendulum motion, the increased speed, the low canine rumble.

They were getting close.

To what?

Antonia, alive and well?

Gravely injured or worse?

All he could do was hold the leash in a death grip, trust
his dog and pray.

FOUR

Catherine's nerves were icy as she sprinted after Garrett and his tugging hound. She refused to let her fear yank her into despair. They would locate her sister alive. And her uncle too. Yet she could not completely banish the flash of memory of finding her father. Would she discover her sister too? Gravely injured? Worse?

Shoulders stiff, she wrestled the fear back into its well-worn channel. *You aren't going to win this time, Stone.*

But when the dog let out an emphatic "woof," her terror ignited.

Pinkerton nosed at a spot to the side of the path as if he might ingest the scent itself. She peered around Garrett's broad shoulder, barely discerning the droplets on the ground, ink-dark. Cold prickles stabbed her all over. It took a moment for her to realize Garrett had half turned to grip her forearm while he hauled the hound to a full stop.

"It's blood, isn't it?" she said before he could get a word out.

He gave one brief nod. "You should go back, wait with Hagerty."

She shook her head as she detached herself from his touch. Was her message clear enough? *You let him escape. You are the reason this is happening.* And there was no way she would flinch from whatever was to come. She would be there for her sister. "Let's go."

He did not need to command Pinkerton, who was again following his nose around the bend in the trail.

Antonia. Antonia. Her sister's name beat against her skull. *You'd better not be dead, you hear me? All that survival training and self-defense stuff you bragged about.* It had to have been enough to save her. Catherine clung to that thought as they jogged. Their pace quickened and it was all Garrett could do to hang on to the leather lead as the dog sped along, ears flapping audibly in the wind.

Pinkerton galloped off the trail, skidding to a stop at the side of a towering granite outcropping. Her view was obscured by his enormous ears and quivering body, and his baying echoed like an air-raid siren.

Garrett went to his knees and she saw. Her sister sat half-propped against the rock, eyes closed, her short hair a platinum corona.

"Tony," she gasped, falling down next to her and grabbing her hand.

Garrett pulled Pinkerton away and ordered him to sit.

Tears blurred Catherine's vision as Garrett sought a pulse. At first his words did not penetrate the excruciating pain in her chest.

"She's alive."

Alive.

Catherine squeezed her sister's cold fingers. "I'm right here, sis. Can you hear me? We're going to get you to the hospital. You'll be okay."

Garrett spoke urgently into his cell phone.

Her sister twitched, then blinked, and Catherine forced down her terror in favor of an encouraging smile. "Tony, it's Catherine. Can you answer me?"

"You know I hate that nickname," she whispered.

Relief made her dizzy. "Sorry." For a moment they both simply breathed, fingers entwined together. "Help is coming. Can you tell me what happened? How did you get out here?"

Antonia blinked again, grimacing. "Porter showed up. I tried to fight him off, but he was too strong. Uncle Orson intervened. He told Stone he'd called the cops and they were headed up the drive, but I think it was a bluff. Stone freaked anyway. He was shoving me into the car when I broke free and ran. I was going to get clear of the house, head for the neighbor's and get help, but I fell and hit my head." She rubbed at her temple. Now her dark eyes, brown like their father's had been, came into focus. "Did he...? Is Uncle Orson...?"

"Missing." She could not bear to say "kidnapped."

A dribble of blood trickled down her sister's cheek from her brow. "Why won't Porter leave us alone?"

If only she had an answer to that question. "The police are looking for him."

Her laugh was bitter. "Oh, great. Super comforting."

Of course, it wouldn't comfort either of them. "We'll get you to a hospital. We'll find him." And Stone would be punished like he should have been a decade before. It had to be that way because the thought of going back into hiding struck her soul like a hammer.

Hagerty arrived with backup a few minutes before the firefighters, who had to carry Antonia to the ambulance on a stretcher after they stabilized her. From what Catherine could see, the source of the bleeding was a cut on her forehead, but who knew what kind of unseen injuries she'd sustained trying to save their uncle?

Garrett gave Pinkerton a handful of treats, which the dog devoured in seconds, trotting along as they hurried back to his car. She wanted to take the wheel herself, speed after the ambulance as it raced away, but they arrived to find a woman and a man on scene, their tall statures and strong chins marking them as Wolfes. The woman was obviously Garrett's twin.

"Stephanie Wolfe," she said, "and this is my brother Chase."

Chase nodded, his hair a mess of wild curls. He was taller and rangier than his siblings. "We'll stay. Get whatever we can from Hagerty."

"Garrett." There was steel in Stephanie's voice. "I need to talk to you privately for a moment."

"Later. Taking Catherine to the hospital."

"Garrett…" she said again, this time through clenched teeth.

Catherine got into the passenger seat. If this family drama was going to play out any longer, she'd ask Hagerty for a ride, but Garrett got in and cranked the ignition. His sister's fury followed them as they left.

"I don't need you to drive me," she said. "Let me borrow your car or get a lift from the cops."

"It's no problem."

"I think it is. Your sister's furious. She doesn't want you involved in this."

"And you don't either, do you?"

She paused. "Do you blame me?"

"No, actually. He got away because of me."

"It's not…" She bit back the comment.

"Not what?"

"I get that things happen. My dad was a cop before he switched to corporate life and I understand it's an impossible job."

"But?" His tawny eyes flicked to hers. "Say it, Catherine."

"You didn't believe us," she blurted. "You refused to accept that Stone was guilty of murdering my father." The anger poisoned her words, hardening them into arrows. "You took his word because he was a local, you knew his dad. Did you let him escape? Turn your back for a minute on purpose?"

He didn't flinch, didn't move, but a vein jumped in his jaw. "No," he said slowly. "I did not. I may have been a failure as a detective, but I had integrity—still do, as a matter of fact."

She knew her comment had cut into him and she was glad. Hurt for hurt. Payback. But she couldn't sustain the flash of anger because she read in his expression that it was true. He hadn't let Stone escape. It had tortured him too, likely. And whatever reason caused him to doubt Stone's guilt, it was a legitimate one, at least in his mind.

I'm sorry, she wanted to say, but the words wouldn't emerge past the mass of emotion roiling in her gut.

They drove the remainder of the way to the hospital in silence, then checked in and settled into uncomfortable waiting room chairs.

The doctor allowed her to see Antonia an hour later.

Garrett shrugged. "I, uh, I'll wait here."

She nodded and hurried in.

"Just bumps and bruises," the doctor pronounced to her profound relief. "I'll give you a few minutes, but the police are waiting to interview her."

Her sister looked small in the big bed, a bandage covering her forehead and dark shadows prominent under her eyes.

She tried for a grin, but her customary fire was missing. Then again, maybe it had dulled long ago. Catherine only saw her sister via video calls and a clandestine face-to-face once or twice a year.

"Fancy meeting you here," Antonia said.

"I never know where you'll turn up." Catherine gripped her hand.

"I don't suppose they caught him? Found our uncle?"

She shook her head. "They will."

"They won't." Antonia shut her eyes and tears trickled from beneath her closed lids. "This is all my fault."

"No, it's not. Don't say that. How could you have known Stone was going to escape again?"

"He never should have even been involved in our lives. I broke up with him after two dates and he turned into a monster after that. I knew when we hiked up to that cabin in Burney it wasn't going to work out between us."

"Like I said, you couldn't have known," Catherine said more firmly.

But when her sister looked at her again, there was an odd detachment in her expression.

"I wish I could believe that, but I know it's my fault, deep down. I'm going to fix it."

Catherine edged close. "No, you're not. Whatever you're thinking, stop it right now."

"You always tried to take care of everyone, me especially, after…" She swallowed, a little sob escaping.

"Listen to me, sis. Stone is the bad guy here. Not you. Promise me you won't get involved, that you'll trust the police to do their jobs."

"Do you?" Spots of color rose on Antonia's cheeks. "Do you think that cop out there—Garrett, I mean—is going to catch him somehow? After he's escaped twice already?"

"Garrett's not a cop anymore, but there are lots of officers involved now. They'll…" Her comment trailed off under her sister's intense scrutiny.

"No one is going to do it, Cath, and you know it," Antonia

said fiercely. "We have to take care of ourselves now that he knows where we are."

Knows where we are... The safety of their fake names and identities would help them no longer. "Tony..." she began when Hagerty poked his head in.

"Sorry to intrude, but I need a statement."

"Have you found our uncle?" Antonia demanded.

He heaved out a breath. "Not yet, ma'am, but we've got the roads covered in and out of town plus the train and bus stations."

She shook her head. "So the answer is no."

He paused. "Correct, ma'am. At the moment we do not know the whereabouts of your uncle or Porter Stone. If I could have your statement, we need to figure out how Stone knew you both were here in Whisper Valley."

Antonia wearily waved a palm. "I don't know, but I'll tell you what I can, which isn't much."

"I'll be outside," Catherine said.

"Can you get me some clean clothes?" Antonia said. "The doctor says I'm getting sprung later today and I can't stand the thought of parading around in my dirty jeans. We can't get into Uncle Orson's house until the cops finish."

Catherine wasn't sure if their uncle's wife, Linda, would let them into the house at all. One problem at a time. "I'll find you something to wear until we can get your things," Catherine promised. Her rental car with her own bag of belongings had probably been confiscated by the police for evidence collection too. At least her ATM card was in her pocket, along with a small amount of cash, enough to buy her sister an outfit.

"I'll be back," she promised, the door closing behind her.

Garrett pushed off the wall where he'd been leaning. "How is she?"

"Bruised and upset. She blames herself." Catherine didn't stop, making for the elevator.

He hustled after her. "Where are you going?"

"To buy her some clothes. She's going home in a few hours." Home? Where exactly was that? Her sister rented an apartment in Portland. She couldn't possibly be going back with their uncle's whereabouts unknown. Where exactly would they stay if Linda didn't allow them to sleep at Orson's place? Was it wise to stay there anyway? It would be a neon sign that the Hart girls were back in town no matter how they disguised themselves. Stone would know exactly where to find them. She suppressed a shiver. "And I need to find us a hotel room."

"I'll drive you."

"No, thank you. I'd rather take a taxi."

"The town knows you, Catherine. The safest thing is to hang on to your Molly identity and lay low until they find your uncle and Stone."

"I'll be fine."

He stopped her, his fingers warm on her wrist. "Please. My family can help."

Her nerves hummed. "I don't need your help and I don't want it."

He did not release her. "I know you don't. I get that. But we have the tools to find people. At least let us…"

She stepped away and into the open elevator. "I said no thank you."

As the closing door shut out the pain in his eyes, an ache started up in her chest.

Garrett didn't deserve her scorn. His failure hadn't been intentional. She'd failed her father too, in her own way, fallen asleep with her headphones on, music blasting like Dad had cautioned her not to do many times. If she'd been able to hear Stone arguing with her father, attacking him, she might have saved him.

Garrett Wolfe's life had also been upended by Stone. She could empathize, but it didn't mean she had to do any more than that. She lifted her chin and stared at the cold metal panels.

He was a temporary ally only.

You're on your own like you've always been.

Did you let him escape? Turn your back for a minute?

Catherine's earlier accusation burned like acid, more so because he'd been investigated after the incident. Cleared, yes, but he could still taste the shame, and humiliation, the fear that he'd see doubt in the eyes of his chief and fellow officers. They'd all taken an invisible step away from him, as if his failure could possibly taint their own careers and reputations.

He returned to the sprawling Security Hounds Ranch, giving Pinkerton an ear rub before he let him loose in the gated yard. Wally, his brother Roman's dog, looked up from the massive hole he was excavating, his torso coated with grime. Stephanie's champion liver-and-tan bloodhound, Chloe, ever fastidious, sprawled in a patch of spring sunshine, completely ignoring her male counterparts.

Garrett knew he was about to face a firing squad, but he trudged inside anyway, the scent of coffee from the perpetually brewing pot making his mouth water. Beth's closed bedroom door indicated she was home from her surgical prep appointment, napping. Napping was a signal that his retired Air Force-nurse mother, who never sat still unless absolutely necessary, was in serious pain.

The surgery had been moved up when a spot in the OR became available. Roman and his new wife, Emery, intended to shorten their honeymoon to hurry back but Beth had thrown a full-on fit, insisting they not alter plans for her. Emery's father, newly exonerated of an attempted murder charge, was relishing his time caring for his grandson, the nephew Emery and Roman were raising that he brought over frequently for Beth to spoil. Things were under control and there was no need for the honeymooners to rush home. That was the party line anyway, and he wouldn't object.

"The pre-op went fine," Stephanie said before he could even ask the question. "She's got a green light for the surgery on Friday morning. She reports Thursday."

"That's good."

She sat on the sofa, crossed one long leg over the other and propped them on the decorative table. "Now that we've gotten the niceties out of the way, care to enlighten me on the reasons for your ridiculous behavior?"

Chase emerged from the hallway with an enormous cup of coffee in his palm. His mop of curls indicated he was overdue for a haircut yet again. "O-o-oh, perfect. We're just in time. Can't wait to hear you try and wiggle out of this one, Garrett."

Their younger sister, Kara, followed him in, barefoot as always. She quietly fixed Garrett a mug of coffee, which he accepted with thanks. At least Kara would try to understand. He knew he wouldn't get quite the same compassionate ear from his other siblings.

He plastered on his usual easy smile and sprawled casually in a leather chair. "Afternoon to you all too."

Kara smiled, but the other two did not. Chase leaned against the wall. "Hagerty says Stone is still at large, no update on the whereabouts of Orson. What's your status report?"

A former Army scout, Chase didn't believe in cluttering up reports with anything other than the vital components.

"Antonia appears to have minor injuries only. She'll be released today. I dropped Catherine in town to buy some clothes for her." He shrugged. "That's what I've got. Figured we could start from there."

"No," Stephanie said calmly. "We should have started earlier, like with a phone call from you where you filled us in instead of barreling into a potentially dangerous situation for a woman concealing her identity, no less."

Kara tucked her feet underneath her and smiled. "We know Molly Hartman is Catherine Hart, daughter of Abe Hart, murdered ten years ago allegedly by Porter Stone."

He appreciated the "allegedly," not surprised that his te-chie sister had already revisited the facts of the case he'd worked on. He took a breath. "No need to be cagey. You already know the rest. Stone escaped on my watch at the ar-raignment because I was trying to arrange a private room to talk to him. Since then he's terrorized the sisters, hence their fake names."

Stephanie folded her arms. "Why didn't Antonia and Catherine involve the police if Stone was threatening them all this time?"

He winced. "Don't exactly blame them. He would likely have been tried and convicted if I hadn't botched things at the arraignment."

Stephanie cocked her head. "So that's what's behind this? Your guilt?"

"Behind what?" From the look on her face it was clear that he wasn't going to distract her from the topic. He stopped her before she could launch in. "Sis, I know. I got involved and I shouldn't have. The smarter thing to do would have been to call the cops and share my suspicion that someone was in her car. But you know what an impulsive, fly-by-the-seat-of-my-pants guy I am, right?"

She raised a finger. "Don't try to charm your way out of this."

"Okay. She needed help. I stepped in."

"Fine. Over and done with and you're out of it, right? Handing this over to the cops?"

He met the challenge she'd fired at him, his smile melting away. "I want to help find Stone. I figure I owe Catherine and Antonia that much, at least."

"The way Catherine was looking at you, I'd say she doesn't want your help," Chase said over the top of his mug. He knew a thing or two about women who wanted to go it alone.

"I'll win her over," he said with a cockiness he did not feel. "Been trying to figure out why Stone returned to Whisper Valley now. Did he know somehow that Catherine and Antonia were here?"

Chase frowned. "Not necessarily. Possibly he needed money and a place to hide. His family's local still. He saw Catherine and grabbed his chance to get to her sister."

"Garrett?" Kara toyed with her thick braid. "What made you doubt Stone was innocent aside from his not-guilty plea? What were you going to question him about at the arraignment before he escaped?"

He stepped back into that awful day, the certainty he'd felt that he'd missed a key detail, that there was something more, just out of his reach. How could he actually say it aloud? "All the evidence pointed to his guilt—his prints in the house, blood on his truck. That's why he was arrested, but I wanted to understand his motive. That's the part I couldn't square."

Kara looked closely. "What was it, Gare Bear? Something in particular bothered you."

When Kara pulled out her nickname for him, he knew she

wasn't going to be diverted either. "Shoes," he said finally. "It was the shoes."

Now his siblings were all staring at him. No going back. "I was questioning Stone's parents, his brother, the neighbors, and I encountered a man who lived in the woods near where Stone parked his tow truck and switched to his personal vehicle for his pizza delivery job. The guy pointed to his boots. Said Stone had taken his own boots off one winter day, insisting the man accept them because his were in tatters." He rolled his shoulders, feeling his cheeks flush. "It just kept bugging me. How does a guy who gives away his own shoes turn to violence over something as trivial as not being allowed to date someone?" Of course, there were tons of reasons. Heat of the moment. Hair-trigger temper. People could love unconditionally in some circumstances and hate passionately in others.

Maybe that's why you didn't make it as a cop. Your brain just can't keep up with reality. The dark cloud settled down on him again, the same one that showered him with self-doubt all those years he'd struggled to read, to write, to cover up the problem that would later be identified as dyslexia. *Maybe you're just not smart enough.*

Kara smiled at him. "That makes sense to me."

No doubt it landed in the ludicrous zone for Chase and Stephanie but they didn't say so. "And they couldn't find any definitive fingerprints from Stone on Abe Hart's wallet taken from his delivery vehicle."

Chase raked the hair from his forehead. "Police report says Abe didn't want Stone dating Antonia. She was too young, sixteen to his eighteen. She went ahead and saw him twice anyway before she decided he wasn't her flavor of the day and broke up with him."

Garrett searched his memory. "Stone's father and mother

had a contentious relationship while he and his brother, Wyatt, were growing up and his reaction was to hide in his room, wait for the argument to die down. He was never confrontational."

"Still waters…" Stephanie said.

"I know. People snap. Stone must have, obviously." Garrett swallowed. "It's clear now that I was wrong about him." Something he'd only recently been able to push from his mind until the moment he'd recognized Catherine. "He escaped from my custody and he's stalked the sisters ever since. How'd he get away from the cops this time?"

Steph consulted her phone. "Last month he was spotted a half hour from here in Durnsville where Catherine and Antonia lived as kids and he was busted. Yesterday they were moving him to a van for transport to a less crowded facility like I told you. They were in the process of recuffing him when he shoved a cop and bolted. No word on how he evaded pursuit."

Garrett groaned. "Now he's got Orson, and Antonia barely escaped."

"Not your fault, nor your responsibility." Stephanie laced her fingers together.

"Yes, it is my fault, which makes it my responsibility." The room went quiet. "I understand it's not a Security Hounds case, but I'm making it mine until Stone is found." Garrett summoned a playful expression that felt like an ill-fitting mask. "Relax, sis. I won't do anything you all wouldn't do."

Stephanie rolled her eyes and sighed deeply. "That's what worries me. We'll help."

Chase nodded. "Already got feelers out. Bill Stone and Wyatt live in the RV park by the river. They still run the tow truck business. Hagerty is aware, so I'm sure they've got eyes on that in case Stone heads there. Where did Porter's mother wind up?"

Kara consulted her phone. "Tracy Stone remarried and moved to Nevada."

"All right, so we'll have to assume Stone didn't make it out of the area before Hagerty got the people in place to watch the exit roads. If he's still here…" Garrett said.

"We'll find him, emphasis on the 'we,'" Stephanie said. "No more blazing a trail on your own."

Garrett quirked an eyebrow. "Or what?"

"Or she'll get out the big guns and tell Mom," Chase said.

Garrett laughed and looked away out the window, pretending he was watching the bloodhounds while he sought composure. He didn't deserve these siblings, who had his back no matter what. He was supposed to be the one who helped them, not the other way around. Finally, he nodded. "All right. But mission number one is getting Mom through her surgery and recovery."

They all nodded.

"Mission number two is to find Porter Stone." Then Garrett added on silently, *And to make sure Catherine and Antonia are safe until he's put away for good.*

FIVE

Catherine kept the conversation at the thrift shop as brief as possible. Small-town curiosity was a real phenomenon and she knew the few patrons thumbing through the racks were tracking her every move. Merely observing a newcomer, or were they on edge from the alert of Stone's escape? She studiously avoided eye contact, pulled down her cap and slid on her glasses, hoping they would not decide to start up a friendly chat. *You're Molly, remember?* Painful though it was, she would hold on to her fake identity a little while longer.

As she handed over her payment for the garments she'd selected, she caught a snatch of conversation from the two women sifting through used paperbacks.

"...how Bill Stone must feel. He lost his wife, one son a fugitive, and the one he's got left milking him for everything."

How Porter's dad must feel? Anger warmed her belly as she strode out. Whatever Bill Stone had lost had been the fault of his own kin, his son's murderous actions. Her father was a complete innocent. As far as "the one he's got left," she could only assume that meant Wyatt. She'd heard bits and pieces from Antonia that the brothers had been close before the murder, sharing an interest in metal detecting and following the same college basketball team.

How did it feel to Wyatt now, to know what his brother

had become? The Stones had once been a seemingly functional family of four, living not far from her uncle. Antonia had actually met Porter when he was working his second job as a pizza delivery guy in Durnsville.

The area was quiet outside. A sporadically traveled main street with an auto repair place, a tiny post office and a coffee shop. There was a trickle of people visiting a business where they could rent gear for river rafting and fishing poles, or snag trail maps of Mt. Shasta. The Klamath River and the area's many lakes provided plenty of fishing opportunities. The region was an adventurer's playground, especially in spring and summer.

Her Uber app showed no available drivers in the vicinity. Not much business in such a rural location. A cab maybe? Yes, there was a company she could call.

She was about to dial her phone when a car pulled up at the curb and a familiar saggy-eared dog shoved his head out the rear window to greet her, slinging a trail of saliva in his excitement. The passenger glass slid down.

"We were in the neighborhood," Garrett called out. "Thought I could give you a lift back to the hospital."

She didn't want to be in the car with him again, but two ladies, their arms laden with shopping bags, were exiting the store, whispering to each other. It felt as though the shoppers, the people on the other side of the street and even those driving by were staring. She found herself reaching for the door and sliding in.

Pinkerton let loose with a throaty yowl of joy that made her chuckle.

Garrett's smile was wide, as if there wasn't a strange and twisted history between them.

"Uh, thank you," she said stiffly.

"My pleasure."

He sounded so sincere, but that was part of his act, she decided. Smooth, funny, self-deprecating Garrett Wolfe. It probably made young women fall in love with him all the time. That husky voice and the crooked smile would surely have snagged her interest too ten years ago, when they'd met, if she hadn't been in shock over her father's murder. The clean scent of his soap made her inhale a little deeper until she corrected herself.

He reached behind the seat and pulled out a cardboard tray holding two steaming cups.

"I owe you a coffee, since we never got around to drinking one at the business meeting."

The meeting from which she'd been abducted and probably would be dead if Garrett hadn't followed her. With gratitude, she accepted one, letting the warm steam soothe her senses. For the second time that day she thanked him. It felt both wrong and right at the same time. After a deep breath she added, "And I should also thank you for following me and intervening at the bridge. I—" She cleared her throat to add more, but he cut her off.

"God put me in the right spot, is all."

His humility, his faith, felt soothing, like the steam rising to warm her cheeks. But she shouldn't feel soothed, not here and now, and especially not with him. He wasn't a cop and he wouldn't be involved in the case going forward. "I'm sorry for what I said, about you letting Stone escape." She couldn't quite look at him while she said it, but she felt his gaze on her.

"I can see how it might have looked like that." His tone was subdued, pained. "If it makes you feel any better, the department put me on leave and investigated."

She did look at him now and the shame on his face was clear before he covered it up with a half smile. "Anyway…

if you need to hear me say it again, I didn't let him go, and if I had that two minutes back, I would never have allowed it to happen."

His sorrow struck a chord and she reached out and took his hand. "I believe that." His fingers gripped hers and the powerful connection she felt shocked her into letting go. This would not do. *Take the ride. Then you'll never see him again. Remember that your uncle's been abducted.*

"Are you all right, Catherine?"

She realized the cup was quivering in her unsteady fingers and Pinkerton was snuffling her hair.

"Yes," she said, managing to get out the single word as she reached up to touch Pinkerton's satin ears. He licked her cheek, and the side of her coffee cup for good measure, before she moved it out of range. "Just eager to get back to my sister."

He put his own coffee in the holder. As he prepared to turn out, his phone rang. After checking the caller ID, he put it on speaker. "I'm here with Catherine, Officer Hagerty. Go ahead."

"An update, and it isn't much," Hagerty said. "Stone didn't turn up at his family's place that we can confirm. Witness saw the vehicle headed north, away from town."

She held the cup tighter to stop the trembling. There were miles of open space to the north, wild rock formations and trees so thick they concealed vast secret canyons. How would they be able to find Uncle Orson? She bit back a groan.

"Going to double back with Antonia with more questions," Hagerty said. "We've sent out BOLOs to the neighboring counties in case Stone slipped by us."

If he had, would she ever see her uncle alive again?

"I'm giving Catherine a ride to the hospital now. We'll meet you there."

"Check in with me. I'm going to make a statement to the press about what went down and I want to try and keep Catherine's name out of it as best I can. We're going to have to get creative and you're the most creative guy I know."

"Thanks... I think."

"You're welcome," Hagerty said, then ended the call.

They drove in silence for a couple of blocks. There was a distinct pink flush to Garrett's cheeks. "I, uh, I was wondering if you and your sister had decided where to stay, or anything."

In fact she'd been wrestling with that very problem. Sticking to her fake name was probably the best way to stay safe, but occupying Uncle Orson's home wasn't. The hotel might be an option, but she'd have to show ID and that would mean handing over her information to a nosy desk clerk.

"I'm not sure yet."

"Maybe—"

"We'll figure it out," she said, cutting him off and drinking too fast from her coffee. Whatever he'd meant to say, she didn't want to hear, especially if it was his offer of help. She and her sister had been going it alone for a decade and that's the way she meant to keep things. "How's your mother?"

He looked surprised. "Nice of you to remember in light of everything that's happened. She's prepared for the surgery, probably nervous, but she'd never let on."

"And you're worried."

"Nah. Not me."

She pointed. "That little groove in your forehead? That's a worry groove."

He laughed. "Is it? I thought it was a distinguished mark of studious thought." He shrugged. "I will admit to a little concern about Mom. It's a complicated surgery and the outcome isn't guaranteed. She's needed it for a long while—her pain escalates every year, but she's always found reasons to put her health on hold to take care of us."

"Beth seems stubborn, like my sister."

Garrett grinned. "Maybe 'determined' is a better word. She has an iron will and a velvet heart."

A return smile crept out of nowhere. She could not help but envy Garrett a little. The center of his world was his family—a loving mother and devoted siblings. There was something so right about that and so rare.

He sighed. "Dad would have been able to convince her to do it."

"How old were you when he died?"

"Fifteen."

Even younger than she'd been when her father was murdered. The sad echo in his words resonated in the empty space her father's death had left inside. She had the strange urge to take his hand again and show him she understood, experience a shared connection with him one more time.

But he has a parent left and you have no one.

Thanks to him.

The thought didn't land right. Why not? She'd blamed Garrett for ten years for letting Stone escape.

But Garrett hadn't taken her father's life. He was simply the one left on whom she'd hung her burden of anger. Him and God. The surprising thought welled up from way down in her spirit and along with it a little extra space to take a deeper breath. It wasn't enough to blow away the resentment and pain, but a sufficient quantity that her ribs expanded for what felt like the first time in years and she felt as if she could look at Garrett and see him better. There was pain in him, and gentleness. Strange, she thought, to notice that.

Now she was practically guzzling the coffee, sifting through the barrage that hit her as they approached the hospital. Emotions she should be feeling, and those she shouldn't. What a muddled mess. After Garrett found a space in the parking structure, he slipped a gray vest with the Security Hounds logo around Pinkerton.

"He's allowed in?"

Garrett clipped a leash to the harness. "Pinky is, and Steph's dog, Chloe. Mom's dog, Arthur, would be welcome anytime as well. Wally, Roman's bloodhound, on the other hand, has been permanently barred from hospital visitations. The charge nurse said if he ever set a paw in the place again, she'd personally take after him with a broom."

"Not well behaved?"

"An unrepentant food scoundrel through and through. I believe there are even wanted posters with his picture in the hospital cafeteria after an unfortunate meat-loaf incident."

She giggled. They made their way to the main building where she saw two police officers talking to the charge nurse. Her stomach knotted. Had they found Uncle Orson? Would it be better to know the truth? Or to live in the uncertain hope that her uncle was okay and Stone had not harmed him?

She was startled when Garrett put a palm on her lower back and urged her forward. "Keep going," he whispered in her ear, and she felt breath-teasing prickles on her neck. Confused, pulse accelerating, she passed him and didn't stop until she joined the people mingling in the lobby.

When she risked a look, she saw Garrett break stride inside the sliding doors as a man appeared with his cell phone outstretched. Pinkerton waggled his bottom in happy greeting and Garrett maintained his warm smile, but she noted the tension in his shoulders.

The man angled his phone toward Garrett.

"Mr. Wolfe, I'm from WKR News."

Her spirit sank. The press. She should have expected it.

"We understand Orson Hart has been abducted from his home."

Garrett nodded. "I heard the same. I'm sure law enforcement is doing all they can."

"An eyewitness saw you at the scene."

She saw Garrett offer a bland smile, appearing totally at ease. "What eyewitness was that?"

"Tom Rudden, an employee for a security company. He also said there were two women there too. Can you confirm that? Were they Orson Hart's nieces? Antonia? Catherine?"

Catherine held her breath as Garrett waved a careless hand. "Sorry. The hound and I are here to visit a friend. You'll have to ask Officer Hagerty about the details."

The reporter was scanning the lobby. "Who was that woman you walked in with?"

Catherine shrank behind a patient shuffling by with her walker.

"A woman?" Garrett said, smile never waning. "Who knows? It's a hospital, right? Lots of people coming and going."

Garrett strode away from the reporter, who hustled to the desk, likely in search of more information. She hoped the staff had been well-trained in privacy matters. Garrett caught her eye as he paused at the drinking fountain and pointed to the elevator, concealing his gesture with his body.

He wanted her to go up to Antonia's floor first, in case the reporter was still watching.

As casually as she could, she entered behind two chatting nurses and pressed the third-floor button. Her tension escalated when the elevator stopped as she expected to see another reporter ready to shove a camera in her face. They'd had enough of that when their father had been killed. All those media hounds, hungry for a story. She had to think of somewhere for her and her sister to go while they awaited word, a place where they'd be out of the public eye.

When she stepped off the elevator, she was startled to see Garrett already there with a panting Pinkerton, who immediately glued his nose to her knee and licked a friendly greeting.

"We took the stairs," Garrett said. "Good exercise."

Pinkerton's tongue lolled from his mouth like an enormous pink ribbon. "I'm not sure your dog agrees."

"Gotta stay in shape to chase those pesky squirrels, buddy." He patted the rust-colored fur.

The nurse behind the desk glanced at Catherine. "Your sister's been asking for you. She got the doctor's all clear. We're working on the discharge papers."

At least that was good news. "Thank you. Can I see her now? I brought her some clothes."

"Sure. She was eating a late lunch. Asked for an extra fruit cup, so that's a good sign."

Catherine pushed through the door. The bed was unoccupied, the sheets tousled, and there was a tray with a crumpled napkin. The bathroom door was closed. Catherine waited a few moments before she tapped. "Hey, sis. It's me. Ready to bust you out of here."

There was no reply so she tapped again, louder, and reached for the handle. The door swung open.

It was empty.

"Garrett," she called.

He and Pinkerton were at her side in seconds.

Catherine looked around helplessly. "She's gone."

He was already on his phone. "Texting Hagerty."

She clutched the bag of clothes, turning in slow circles, trying to imagine what had happened. A deep cold seeped into her. "Stone must have taken her."

"I don't think so."

She jerked a look at him. "How do you know?"

The nurse poked her head in. "Something wrong?"

"Antonia's gone. Do you know where?"

"Not a clue. I didn't see her leave but I was busy with another patient."

Garrett eyed the bedside tray. "What was delivered for her lunch?"

The nurse appeared puzzled.

He pointed. "What was on the tray?"

"Ham sandwich, a fruit cup and container of chicken noodle soup, a chocolate pudding. She requested bottled water, so we found one of those too."

Catherine understood now. There were no empty containers left. What's more, the top bed blanket was missing, as was one of the two pillows from the bed along with Antonia's dirty jeans. "She packed the food and took it along with the water bottle. And she sent me on an errand to get me out of the way."

The nurse frowned. "Why would she do that?"

It's my fault. I'm going to fix it. Catherine's pulse hammered.

Garrett bent to look directly at her. "Catherine?"

"She blames herself for what happened to Uncle Orson."

He let out a long slow breath. "She's gone to find Stone herself, hasn't she?"

Catherine could only nod and hold back the tears.

SIX

Garrett snatched the remaining pillow off the bed and lowered it for Pinkerton.

The dog's tail whipped as he nosed it. Pinky was bounding for the door before Garrett got the command out.

"Stay and wait for Hagerty," he called to Catherine as he raced after Pinky to the stairwell. She clattered down behind him in spite of his request. Catherine would not stand on the sidelines while her sister was rushing off on a fatal mission.

And it would likely be fatal if she found Stone. He outmatched her for desperation and cunning, and if she thought she could confront him that would be her deadliest mistake.

It was all he could do to hold on to the leash and keep on his feet as the bloodhound cannonball descended the stairs. The bottom presented a choice: the main lobby doors out to the parking area or the exit leading to the multilevel garage. Oblivious to the curious stares from those in the lobby, Pinkerton did not hesitate before he hustled to the primary exit. The automatic doors parted just in time to keep the dog from smacking into them.

They bustled into the slanting rays of the setting sun. The U-shaped drive was empty save for a valet handing over the keys to a man loading his wife and newborn into the back seat of a sedan.

Catherine spun around as Pinkerton sank dejectedly on his haunches. "She got into a car?"

"Unfortunately, yes. Pinky's lost the trail." He motioned the parking attendant over. "Did you see a woman leave a moment ago? Blond hair? Carrying a bundle?"

The valet pushed back his baseball cap and nodded. "Uh-huh. She was in a real hurry. Hopped into a cab about twenty minutes ago."

Catherine blew out a breath.

"Which direction?" Garrett asked.

He pointed.

"Thanks." Garrett dialed Hagerty. "Antonia's in a cab, headed north. No indication of her destination."

"Copy that. Over to me then. She hasn't broken any laws, but we'll try to stop her before this gets any worse, at least ask if she'll share her plans."

Garrett signed off. He patted Pinky and gave him a treat. The dog gulped it down and rolled onto his back, paws pedaling the air.

Catherine kneeled and supplied the dog with a satisfying tummy rub.

"You did your best, Pinkerton." Her face was pale and he caught the sheen of impending tears. He touched her arm.

"I'm sorry, Catherine. We'll find her."

"Before she finds Stone?"

It was a question and a challenge all at once.

"I'll do my absolute best. Security Hounds will also." *If you'll allow it.*

She stood, arms folded, staring at the pavement. "My uncle's kidnapped and now Antonia's run off. I don't know what to do."

She was so vulnerable, so small against the hulking building behind her and the growing shadows all around. He could not resist wrapping his arms around her. Her head rested on his chest and he enjoyed the weight of it. "Let's go back to the ranch. Brief the family. Get something to eat. If you don't want to stay there, I'll help you find a hotel room."

Her shoulders stiffened for a moment and before he had a chance to release her, she pressed her cheek against him. "I'm scared." It was both a whisper and a plea.

His heart pounded and he pressed his face to her soft hair. "I know. I would be too. But you're not alone in this. I—I know I let you down in the past, but my family is the best. You can trust them." *Even if you can't trust me.* "Besides," he said when she moved away and swiped at her tears, "Pinky would be crushed to miss out on any more of your expert belly rubs."

The faintest of smiles quirked her mouth. Victory.

Another fifteen minutes passed. With no further word from Hagerty, they headed for the elevator to the garage. Catherine lagged as if she was exhausted. They took it slow.

The doors opened at the first floor where Garrett had parked and they stepped out. Garrett's skin prickled. He stopped Catherine with a finger to his lips. He reached for the Glock he'd been carrying in his side holster since they'd encountered Stone near the hiking bridge. His fingers touched the cold metal as the silent seconds ticked by. No sound of another car or footsteps, only the faint traffic noises from the street. He eyed the half wall of cement that separated the upward lanes from the downward ones. No sign of movement.

Pinkerton flapped his ears. No indication he'd noticed anything either. Pinkerton was strictly a tracking and trailing dog but he usually knew when someone was approaching before Garrett did.

Nothing.

He offered a smile. "Sorry. Nervous Nellie here, I guess."

She didn't answer, keeping pace with him as he hurried them toward his car.

He stepped to the passenger side, bumping into her as she did the same.

"Oh…sorry," she said. "It's been a long time since someone opened the door for me. I can get it myself."

He wasn't sure what to say to that. "My mom trained us to open doors unless otherwise instructed."

"That's sweet. Thank you."

Sweet. He'd take it. Illogical how pleased he felt. With a flourish he reached for the handle again, thumb on the unlock button.

Pinkerton's head jerked to the side.

From the shadows, a car hurtled at them.

The gray SUV stolen from Uncle Orson's garage.

He had only a second to make out the driver—Stone, his knuckles white on the steering wheel. He roared up quickly, stopping so close there was not enough clearance to open the door and bundle Catherine inside.

"Underneath." He helped her slide under his car with Pinkerton. He aimed and squeezed off a shot, which punched through the front window, off center.

Stone got out and ducked low behind his open driver's door.

Pinkerton's barks echoed and bounced through the cement space.

"Hold," he commanded. *Stay with Catherine.* He prayed he would not have to shoot again, but he would do what was necessary to protect them.

"I just called Hagerty, Stone," he shouted. "He's on-site. You'll be caught in moments."

Stone grunted. "Where is she? Her room's empty. Saw you tracking with the dog. Did she sneak out?"

"Who?" Garrett asked, stalling.

"You know who. Antonia."

Garrett countered, "Why don't you tell me where you've got Orson?"

Stone licked his lips. "Put your gun down and I will."

"You fooled me once, Stone," Garrett said. "Not going to happen again."

"That's rich but I don't have time to go into it. I want Antonia, not Orson. He's just the insurance."

Garrett's nerves snapped tight. "Did you hurt him?"

"Stop stalling. Where is she?" The dog barked louder. "I was in the parking lot. I saw her speed off in a cab. Catherine knows where she's headed. Get her out from under the car."

"You don't want this to get any worse, Stone," Garrett said. Pinkerton whined and wriggled, nails scraping the floor.

"My life can't get any worse. I got nothin' to lose and you're going to tell me where to find Antonia or her sister's gonna. One or the other."

"You aren't in the power position here. I'm armed, the cops are responding. You're not getting anything from me."

Stone grabbed something from his pocket, took several steps back and held it up. "Know what this is?"

His stomach dropped at the sight of the flash-bang grenade. It was a nonlethal weapon, but it would incapacitate them all. "Yes, I do," he said slowly. "Where'd you get that?"

"Got it off the cop I decked when I escaped." He continued to back up. "Don't reach for the car door handle or I'll blow it. Hear me?"

"Not smart. It will knock you out too."

Stone laughed. "I'm not stupid, Garrett, like you and your cop buddies all think I am. I didn't stay a free man for ten years by making dumb mistakes."

Garrett spoke louder, sweat prickling his forehead. "You don't need to do this, Porter. It's not going to serve any purpose. We can't tell you where Antonia is because we don't know. The grenade isn't going to change that fact. She took off."

"No. You know where she went."

"He's telling you the truth," Catherine called from under the car. "My sister was gone when we got here and I didn't know anything about her plans."

Garrett tried to push Catherine back with his foot. Remaining beneath the car was her best protection. "Stay under there," he muttered low.

"You're both liars anyway," Stone said. Now he'd edged completely behind the car he'd arrived in, widening the distance between them.

Garrett shook his head, desperately hoping to hear Hagerty's approach. "It's the honest truth. You can check. I'll dial the nurse's desk right now for you. She'll tell you Antonia left before we spoke to her."

"Don't bother." Stone spat the words. "I guess we'll do it the hard way. I'll go to Plan B. A quick flash-bang and I'll take Catherine as bait. Antonia will come to me to save her precious sister and her uncle. A nice tidy package. Better than all this chasing." His smile was feral in the dim light of the garage. Where had the young man gone that Garrett had known? Or thought he had anyway.

"I don't want to shoot you, Stone. Don't make me do that." He meant every syllable. It was the absolute last resort and he'd do anything to avoid it.

Anything but hand over Catherine.

Stone's smile widened. "See that's the thing, right? I thought I wanted to be a cop once upon a time, remember? You were giving me advice. I know cops are trained to look past the target, assess what's beyond, make sure there's no collateral damage. If you took a shot from that distance, it'd ricochet. Could hit some innocent visitor come to collect their car."

"Now who's stalling?" Garrett said.

But Stone was right. He could make the shot, but the light was dim and he could hear the elevator whirring, indicating someone might be stepping onto their floor at any moment.

A sound snagged his attention—another car coming, the whine of a siren louder and louder. Pinkerton joined in until the din was bouncing all over the garage.

Finally. The cops.

Stone heard it too. In one fluid motion, he leaped behind the cement wall.

Garrett had no time to react as Stone lobbed the grenade.

There was a bang so loud it slammed Catherine up against the underside of Garrett's car before it dumped her onto the floor again. Vaguely she felt Garrett collapse nearby, his crumpled body making no noise as it fell. Pinkerton went still next to her.

Confusion, a splitting pain in her skull, the feeling that her eardrums had exploded... She tried to reach for Garrett but she couldn't move. Her vision darkened, spiraling inward until she could see only a small spot, a pinprick of light. Had she been struck blind by the explosion? A piercing ringing in her brain deadened all her other senses.

Move, she told herself. *Stone's out there and he's coming. You've got to get Garrett, Pinky and go.*

All her effort produced no response except a slight curling of one hand. She was paralyzed. Her terror escalated rapidly when fingers wrapped around her ankle. She tried to scream, crawl, kick, but her body wasn't working right.

From deep in her stupor she realized it must be Stone. He was maneuvering to get a better hold to pull her out. She tried to yank away, but she couldn't fight off the effects of the explosion. From inside a thick cloud she felt Stone tugging at her arm. With the heavy dog on one side and Garrett's body blocking his access, he only succeeded in moving her a few inches. She wanted to resist, to call out for help, but her mouth refused, her brain slow and sluggish.

Garrett hadn't moved. Was he unconscious? Worse? Her pulse skittered.

The tugging continued. Now he'd snagged a fistful of her jacket. Inexorably, he was sliding her away from Pinkerton and Garrett.

Stone was going to take her and she was helpless to resist.

Despair clawed at the edges of her mind. Her father was dead. Her sister and uncle, gone. And now Stone would have her too.

Fight back, Catherine. Come on.

She managed to turn her head and with every iota of strength she could muster, she bit Stone on his wrist. He let go, but only for a moment. After he repositioned, he got one hand on her neck, careful to keep out of biting range.

New plan. She'd try to wedge herself against the tire as he pulled her out, making it as hard on him as she possibly could.

But then another sensation pushed through her stupor, a vibration through the cold floor. And then the grip on her ankle was suddenly gone. She blinked hard as her vision expanded in painfully small increments. The wailing in her ears abated. It required several calming breaths to reassure herself she was alive and still safe under Garrett's car.

Garrett?

Was he okay?

Pinkerton?

She tried to move her hand, to find the dog's furry side in the darkness, but she couldn't. She was completely helpless, now at the mercy of whomever had arrived.

She prayed it was Hagerty. That he'd come in time to capture Stone. End the nightmare for her family.

But was it too late for Garrett and Pinky?

God, please don't let them be hurt.

God? she thought in her haze. Her brain told her it was a wasted plea.

But her heart insisted.

God, help them, she prayed again. It was the first time in a long while that she'd prayed for anyone outside the tattered remains of her family circle. Somehow it felt right. She knew Garrett would think so too.

Hagerty's worried face appeared around the tire. Her body shivered with relief. His lips moved, but she could not hear whatever he was saying. It was as if she was underwater. When he eased her from beneath the car, she saw Garrett had been placed on his back, another cop kneeling at his side. She could not see blood, but he was completely still. She suspected the noise had caused him to fall backward into the car and strike his head, like she had.

"Is he okay?" She felt her lips move but she didn't hear anything come out. Hagerty did not react to her question. He was alternately talking urgently into his radio and speaking to the arriving medics.

Pinkerton was lying on his tummy between her and Garrett, stocky legs sprawled out at ungainly angles. His nose twitched and he stretched out a paw toward Garrett.

At least the dog was alive. He let loose with a howl that was so piteous, it actually penetrated her deadened ears.

She understood the fearful question twined in Pinkerton's agonized cry.

Was Garrett Wolfe alive or dead?

Hot tears left warm trails down her cheeks. A uniformed medic loaded Garrett onto a stretcher. Pinkerton lurched up and pawed at Garrett's legs. The dog was trembling now, snaking his long pink tongue up to lick his master's still face.

Hagerty helped a second medic load Catherine onto another and she was whisked toward the hospital that had just treated her sister.

Stone had won again, she thought until she corrected herself.

No. Thanks to Garrett, Stone hadn't prevailed.

But he'd come close, so close, and this time he'd endangered anyone who might have been nearby in the parking garage.

When would it end?

She smothered her desire to cry.

Stone hadn't won.

But if she didn't find her sister soon, he just might.

SEVEN

Garrett's senses returned in a whoosh of panic in the hospital room.

Catherine...where was she? Pinky? His cell phone was missing, he was garbed in a ridiculous hospital gown and his skull throbbed. He grabbed for the blanket to toss it off, but someone stopped him.

Chase.

His brother said something, but Garrett didn't catch it so Chase grabbed his chin, leaned close and began speaking, presumably in a louder volume.

"Catherine is okay. Pinkerton is okay. You are okay, even though you look like you're circling the drain. Did I cover all your immediate questions?" Chase asked.

The relief was sweet. Catherine and Pinky had not been harmed. Garrett sagged. "I've got bongo drums playing in my ears."

"Yeah, that's probably why you're using your outdoor voice. Take it down a notch, would you?" He pointed to Garrett's skull and enunciated in an exaggerated fashion. "Mild concussion from your fall, abrasions. If you're nauseous, that should go away soon. Flash-bang grenades do a number on a person. Am I right?"

He would have nodded if his cranium wasn't about to explode. "Catherine…?"

"Mostly the same as you, but no concussion. Doc says your ears will recover sooner or later."

"Where's Pinky?"

Chase winced and Garrett tried to adjust his volume before repeating the question.

"Steph hustled him to the vet while I stayed with you. Doc Buzzy said he's okay, but he's probably got a headache and he's *really* annoyed that she wouldn't let him stay with you. Silly dog actually refused to get out of Steph's car at the animal hospital. Took Steph, Doc Buzzy and a vet tech to drag him out."

Garrett gaped. Pinkerton was the most relaxed, obedient dog he'd ever trained. The thought of him throwing a fit at being separated from Garrett made a lump form in his throat. Dogs were incredible, a lesson he relearned every day. "But he's not hurt? You're sure?"

"Totally."

The next question he already knew the answer to, but he asked anyway. "Hagerty didn't get Stone?"

Chase shook his head. "Nope. Took off in Orson's car a moment before Hagerty arrived, but we're thinking he must be hiding close by. Has to be if he's concealing Orson and the cops have the highway buttoned up. We're working that angle."

Garrett sorted through his muddied brain. "So I've been here…"

"Overnight. It's Thursday morning."

"I was under that long?"

"On and off. You don't remember our sparkling conversation?" he said with a yawn. "I'll go over it again when you get sprung from here."

Garrett tossed off the covers. "I'm springing myself. Now."

Chase shrugged. "Yeah, I figured. Mom said I was to threaten you with disinheritance but that seems like a waste of effort."

Garrett forced his thoughts to attend. Thursday, a very important day. "She's checked in for surgery?"

"Yes. Good thing we were able to report that you and Catherine were completely fine, otherwise she'd have canceled. Believe me, it took all of us to prevent that happening. She's actually at the end of the hallway, on the other side of Catherine's room. She will be displeased to hear of your self-discharge."

"I'll see her after I check on Catherine."

"Try not to shout, huh? Women don't like that." Chase handed him his cell phone.

Garrett lowered his volume again. "I'll remember. Is my car still in the garage?"

"Yeah. Undamaged. Cops finished with it while you were still in here napping. I'll have the valet park it out front and I'll follow along behind back to the ranch. Just in case."

Just in case. The ranch would be the safest place, the only place, for Catherine to be. He wasn't sure he could convince her, but maybe after the flash bang, she'd be more willing.

I'll take Catherine... Antonia will come to me to save her sister and her uncle. A nice tidy package. Better than all this chasing. Stone had gotten away, but there was no question in Garrett's mind that he hadn't abandoned his goal.

Chase tossed Garrett's clothes on the bed, along with his phone. "Wait for you downstairs."

It felt strange getting dressed and leaving the room without Pinkerton. The nurse tried to discourage him from going but he simply patted her arm and thanked her for the care, then walked to Catherine's room, trying not to jostle his splitting skull any more than necessary.

Catherine was sitting on the chair, fully dressed, fingering the scrape on her cheek. His heart lurched when she looked at him, eyes like agates. She stood slowly.

"Are you okay?" they said at exactly the same moment.

They both laughed and clutched their heads, which made them laugh more.

"Ugh. No more laughing." She gestured for him to sit on the bed. "You look worse than I feel."

"And here I thought I was Mr. Stoic."

"Mr. Stoic, I owe you. Are we shouting at each other?"

"Possibly."

Her grin brought out the dimple next to her mouth. She tipped her chin, the smile fading away. "You tried to shield me."

"Not enough, was it?"

"Best anyone could have done." She swallowed and he saw the delicate muscles of her throat contract. "Pinky?"

"Is fine, from what Chase tells me." He felt suddenly awkward, sitting like a little kid on the hospital bed, so he stood. "You should…"

She held up a palm. "Please. If you're going to tell me I should stay here overnight again, you'll be a massive hypocrite since you're obviously leaving. I would have left earlier but…"

"But…?"

She shrugged, cheeks pinking. Because she'd been worried about him? Not likely.

"If you want to change your mind and stay, I will too. But I'll be sitting right outside on an uncomfortable hallway chair." He'd meant for a joke, surprised at how much vehemence he'd infused into the words. His soul felt attached to her in that moment, as if her departure might cause him physical pain. He blinked hard to refocus. "Er, my mom's having surgery in the morning so I could kill two birds by staying, so to speak."

"Bad choice of words."

He sighed. "Yes. I'm not at the top of my game."

"Me neither." She looked past him, out the window. "Tony texted me. Apparently, she got out of the cab somewhere close. Probably she didn't have enough cash on her to go any further." She held out her phone to show him the exchange.

Catherine, what happened? I heard the sirens and an explosion.

Stone almost got us in the hospital garage but we're okay. He was looking for you.

Are you sure you're okay?

Yes. You have to come back.

No. He'll stay close because he wants me and he's got Uncle Orson. I know his favorite spots nearby. I'll find him before he finds me.

Catherine sighed. "Why won't she listen to reason? I have no idea where she's headed."

"We'll talk it over with my sibs. They know the area inside and out."

"But you'll want to be with your mother."

"There are four of us, five when Roman gets back. We can do both. Besides, I know my mom would never condone leaving you after everything that's happened." It felt easier to hide behind his mother at that moment. *Hiding? Really, Garrett?* He took a breath. "Come stay at Security Hounds, at the ranch."

She was shaking her head when he added, "Please. We need to plan, which is going to take time. My head is killing me and if I've got to worry about you, it's only going to get worse."

She squirmed and drew a hand through her wavy hair. The tiny furrow in her brow tugged at him and he plowed on. "If you need your own space, Roman's trailer is empty. He moved out after he got married. Bought a house in town for him, Emery and his lug of a dog, if you can believe it. Something about wanting privacy. As if we're a nosy clan or something." He added an elaborate eye roll, which sparked a whole new wave of pain.

She lifted her chin, wincing. "All right. I'm too uncomfortable to argue. Only for a night." She gripped the chair to get up and he offered his arm before he could second-guess it.

She took it and squeezed him close for a moment. "Thank you, Garrett. I really mean that."

His insides tumbled around and he wondered at his reaction. Happiness at being able to right his mistakes by helping her? The concussion playing with his emotions? "My pleasure." Why did it feel like he really meant that too?

They made their way to his mother's room. Catherine expressed her intention to wait outside while he checked in, but Beth called them both in.

"I want to lay eyes on you." Her own eyes were shadowed with pain and worry. "Tell me what the doctor said. Both of you. Full report, right now. I've badgered the charge nurse but she's standing on patient confidentiality."

They each offered an overview until she was satisfied. "And the case?"

He explained about Antonia's departure. "Stone's at large. We'll search for Antonia. Help locate Orson too if the opportunity arises."

Beth frowned. "But Antonia is the first priority because Stone intends to abduct Catherine to force Antonia's hand?"

Garrett nodded. "He said as much."

His mother was silent for a moment before fixing her gaze on Catherine. "I know you're independent, and you have a lot at stake, but you need to let Security Hounds take the lead."

Catherine met her gaze, shoulders squared. Two forceful, determined women. Beautiful, he thought.

"Respectfully, Mrs. Wolfe, I will do what I have to for my family."

"The logistics are best left to the experts. It's what we do."

"To you it's a case. To me it's everything. Would you trust your everything to someone else?"

Beth tilted her head, quiet for a moment. "What you're implying is you'll do what you have to do, even if it's contrary to the team's direction."

Catherine's silence spoke eloquently.

After another beat, his mother continued. "You're willing to take risks, dangerous risks, to rescue your people. I'm asking you not to, for the sake of mine."

"That's an easy ask because you have your family safe right now." Catherine's tone was brittle. "Mine is either dead, abducted or on the run. Imagine how that feels."

Beth sounded sorrowful when she answered. "I won't even try. I am so sorry for what's happened."

Catherine swallowed audibly. "Thank you, and I won't ask your family to risk their safety to help me."

"Garrett will whether you ask or not."

A flush warmed his cheeks.

Catherine's mouth tightened. "I won't let him, or anyone else."

"Mom, it's time for us to go." Every moment they lingered, Antonia might be slipping farther away.

Catherine reached out for Beth's hand. "I'll pray for your surgery to be a success." The words sounded tentative, as if she hadn't known she was going to say them.

Beth smiled. "Thank you. I'll count on that. And you know we are all praying for your uncle and sister."

Catherine ducked her chin and walked out of the room.

He kissed his mom on the brow, banishing the worrying thoughts that crept into his mind when he considered her upcoming surgery.

She touched his hand. "You've made peace with what happened at the arraignment, son. You aren't a cop anymore because God had other things in store. Don't forget it."

Her words pricked at him. He'd fought long and hard to forgive himself, to remember that he was not a failure in God's eyes or his family's. But the nagging ache bubbled up before he could brace against it. He'd let down Catherine and any others Stone had hurt. He'd failed them all.

"I love you, Mom," he said.

"Love you too, Garrett. Keep me posted."

He agreed, but he knew he and his siblings would all be curating what information they provided his mother, so she could finally focus on herself. It would be a juggling act for sure.

The nurse came in and Garrett moved to the door.

"Just one more thing," Beth called. "I don't need, or want, to be babysat here. Finding Antonia and Orson, and protecting Catherine, are the most important things right now. If I hear that any of you is performing a vigil at this hospital for me, I will personally call Security and have you escorted out. Do you hear me?"

"Loud and clear, ma'am." He blew her a kiss and caught up to Catherine at the elevator.

She rounded on him.

"I've changed my mind. I'll stay at Uncle Orson's place. I just need to clear it with Linda."

He huffed out a breath. "There's no need—"

"Your mother is right, Garrett. I'm going to do what I need to for my family, whether or not Security Hounds agrees. I don't want you risking yourself or your siblings."

He clasped her forearm. "We are investigators, not untrained laypeople. We're all expert dog handlers, licensed to carry weapons. It's what we do."

She pulled away. "I don't… I don't want you to get hurt."

He hid the surge of emotion with a flashy smile. "Then we're in agreement. I don't want me to get hurt either." Wrong, to cheapen the moment with humor, to derail the sincerity of what she'd said. He hadn't known how to react so he'd defaulted to the familiar. *Way to go, Garrett.*

She didn't return his smile. "I don't need you taking care of things because you feel guilty about what happened."

He felt a flicker of anger. She thought she knew him well enough to read his motivation? He wasn't the younger version of himself and he knew God had more in store for him when he put down the badge. He resisted the urge to laugh it off. "Maybe I'm involved because it's the right thing to do and it's my business as an investigator. I'm here to do what I can for other people who need me. Right now, that's you. I don't see anyone else around waiting to step in."

He regretted the statement immediately. Pointing out her vulnerability was mean. There had to be a middle ground between laughing things off and hammering people with the truth. They stepped onto the crowded elevator. He scanned each occupant closely. It would be brash for Stone to double back and infiltrate the hospital again to snatch Catherine, but he didn't rule it out.

After discussion with the other people, he kept his neck on a swivel as they exited the lobby into the overcast morning. She was silent as they walked to the front to find his car.

Chase leaned against his own vehicle and gave them a lazy salute.

Her gaze flicked around and he knew she was recalling their terrifying encounter with Stone, wondering where her sister was and if she was safe. He'd no right to condemn her feelings, her desire to act independently, not after what she'd experienced.

He stopped her with a hand on her shoulder. "Look. At least come to the ranch and let us make a plan to assist with the search. Four of us with our obsessive bloodhounds can track much more efficiently than you can. If you want to stay at Orson's, I understand, though it will blow your cover. We can make sure the security system is operable, at least."

She hesitated. "That might work. I'll need to check with my aunt Linda. They're separated, but it's still her home too, but… I can do that later. Is that enough of a compromise?"

His smile was sincere now. "Yes." He offered a palm. "Partners for the moment?"

She didn't exactly smile, but the corners of her mouth did quirk as she shook. "Partners for the moment."

They buckled in and peeled away from the curb, Chase following. Catherine stared resolutely out the window. He knew what she must be thinking.

Where was her sister? Her uncle?

And where was Stone?

EIGHT

The clouds massed into an oppressive wall as she and Garrett left the hospital. She puzzled over the easiness with which she'd offered to pray for Beth. She'd felt like her prayer life had all but ended when she lost her father, but here she was, deciding to pick up the conversation with God again, as if she'd hadn't had Him on hold for a decade. Why was it okay now, to talk to the God who did not save her father? She wasn't sure, but somehow it was.

The countryside should have been soothing, as the tall, waist-high grass, green from winter rains, swished alongside the narrow road. But she wasn't at ease. From behind every tree, hidden in each tangle of bushes, she looked for her sister, or Stone. Her only hope was that they'd stay out of each other's path.

Garrett glanced in the rearview. Chase had not yet made the turn, his vehicle requiring a slower pace to tackle the twisty terrain. She tried to fight the overwhelming weariness that crept along her limbs. Would the day end without news of her loved ones? Or would she get word that Tony or Orson had been found…dead? She felt Garrett looking at her.

"I'm sorry. This must feel like the world is falling apart on you."

"It does. I was excited to come to Whisper Valley. I thought

I was going to start a new job and be able to live a normal life without being afraid of Stone." She firmed up her trembling voice. "Now he's free again and I have to worry about my sister and uncle too. It's like a total reversal."

His gaze caught hers for a moment. His expression was pained and sympathetic. Surprising how much he appeared to actually care. His attention was caught by something over her shoulder and his mouth dropped open.

Adrenaline spiking, she whirled in time to see her uncle's SUV part the grass, roaring up from the tree-lined border, Porter Stone behind the wheel.

Garrett slammed the brakes but there was no way to avoid the collision. The SUV plowed into the rear passenger door of Garrett's car, forcing it forward in a juddering rush. She screamed as they were pinned against a thick tree, metal crumpling around them.

Stone leaped out of his vehicle.

Garrett went for his gun, but Stone rushed at them, a brick in his raised fist. He brought it down on her passenger window, smashing a hole in the glass. She screamed as bits rained down on her.

Before Garrett could free the pistol from the holster, Stone reached in and grabbed her around the throat. "I'll break her neck if you draw."

Garrett froze. "Let her go."

Stone squeezed, impeding her breathing. She clawed at his arms, but he didn't relent.

"I mean it."

Garrett slowly let go of his weapon. "Don't hurt her."

Stone's breath was hot on her cheek. "Where's Antonia?"

"She doesn't know where her sister is," Garrett snapped. "Like I told you in the garage."

Stone tightened his grip. "Give me Tony's cell number. Now."

Catherine struggled to breathe.

"I'll get it," Garrett said. "I'm reaching for the phone in her pocket, okay?"

No, Catherine tried to say. *Don't give it to him.* Her fingernails clawed at his forearms but they were strong as iron bands.

A shot sailed over the roof of the car and Stone immediately released her. Eyes streaming, she watched Stone dive for the SUV, throw it into Reverse and skid into a U-turn on the grass.

Chase raced up, weapon drawn, and aimed at the car for a second shot.

"Don't shoot," she screamed. "He might have my uncle in the trunk."

Chase darted a frustrated look at her as the SUV disappeared into the trees.

"I was going to take out the tires," Chase said.

Garrett clasped her arm. "Are you hurt?"

Her throat was throbbing and her heart pounded so hard her whole body shuddered. Terrified. Traumatized. Desperate but not physically hurt. If she'd been alone though... She pulled in oxygen and forced herself to answer. "No. Not hurt."

His touch was warm, keeping her from losing it completely. "Just breathe. That's all you need to do right now."

Chase dashed off a text, probably to Steph. "I suggest we get out of here before he tries again. Your vehicle is far enough off the road that it won't cause an accident, but I'll put up an emergency cone anyway."

Catherine shook the glass shards off her lap, ignoring the cold wind funneling through the broken window. It didn't come near to matching her inner chill anyway. Garrett slid to the back seat, kicked at the rear door until it grudgingly opened and climbed out. He helped her free from the wreck. With a delicate touch, he whisked away the remaining bits of glass and held her arm while they walked to Chase's car.

He guided her into the rear seat. "We could…"

"If you're going to say go to the hospital, that's not necessary. I'm not hurt, just shaken up."

"But…"

She held up a finger. "Would you convince Steph to go if she was in my position?"

"Uh, no. She'd decline in no uncertain terms."

Catherine nodded. "There you go then."

Chase rejoined them and both men kept shooting wary glances at her in the rearview mirror. She couldn't help but look for Stone around every turn all the way to the Security Hounds Ranch. The heavy cloud cover promised more turbulent weather. Would Antonia be wandering in the elements? Would Stone?

He seemed unstoppable, but she couldn't think that way. He would be stopped. Her family's lives depended on it.

When they arrived, the door flew open and Pinkerton shot out onto the porch and launched himself at Garrett, who almost went down under the assault. He hadn't seen his master since Garrett had been carted away in an ambulance. Catherine laughed as he struggled to maintain his footing and calm the enormous animal.

"Easy, Pinky Pie. I'm in one piece, for the moment anyway."

After finishing his affectionate takedown of Garrett, Pinky trotted over and gave her a more gentle greeting.

"Hello, my friend." And suddenly as she kneeled next to him, tears blurred her vision. This lovely dog had sniffed out her sister's trail, sheltered Catherine under the car, been worried sick about his human partner, who'd stepped into the void for her. It was startling to feel...what was the word? Attached...to a dog and a man who seemed to be trying very hard to help her. And connected in some small way to God. Connectedness was something she'd lost the moment she'd found her father murdered. It was as if in that terrible bloody moment God had reached down and snipped the threads that bound her to others.

Not God.

Porter Stone.

Now as the murmured greetings surrounded her, she felt as if those threads were being knotted together again. She was not sure how to feel about it. It was certainly not the moment for any kind of community-building with what she'd just experienced. She caressed Pinky again before she straightened.

They gathered at the kitchen table—Kara, Stephanie, Chase, Garrett and her.

"Are you sure you're okay, Catherine?" Kara said.

Catherine tried not to show the tenderness in her muscles as she nodded and slipped into the offered chair. Rain began to splatter the kitchen window.

Kara slid a platter of muffins, studded with blueberries, in front of her. Chase poured mugs of coffee and quirked an eyebrow at the treats.

"Are these more of your weeds-and-seeds muffins, Kara?"

"Yes, and you're going to love them like you do all my weeds-and-seeds recipes." Kara shrugged and looked at Catherine. "Chase teases me for being a vegan, but I don't see him turning up his nose at my cooking."

Chase grinned and snagged a muffin.

Catherine found that despite everything, she was ravenous

and took one herself. If it was made of weeds and seeds, it was a delicious combination. "Wonderful," she said. "Thank you."

Kara nodded. "I like to keep the team fueled up, especially when Mom isn't around."

"Hagerty told me where the cab dropped Antonia, and I took Chloe. She got a trail briefly but lost it. Antonia must have hitched a ride from someone."

"With Antonia on the loose and Porter determined to use Catherine to get to her, we've got double the danger," Garrett said. "Two targets with a lot at stake, not to mention Orson's situation. Could this get any more complicated?"

"Umm, as a matter of fact..." Kara said.

What now? Catherine tried to not to groan aloud as she waited for the next shoe to drop.

Garrett swiveled a look at his youngest sibling.

Kara paused. "I sort of went off on a bunny trail, because something was bothering me about the abduction scene at Orson's. The fact that the security system was offline. Convenient, right? The fellow was there to service it at the moment Stone happened to show up to abduct Orson?"

"That was bothering me too," Garrett said. "Did you find any connections?"

"Rudden's worked for Orson for eleven years or so. There's nothing to indicate they had any kind of contentious relationship, but..." Kara suddenly became focused on the untouched muffin in front of her. "It might be a little awkward for you, Catherine."

"If it helps Tony, I'll accept awkward."

Kara's cheeks turned a delicate pink. "It's all gossip, of course, hearsay. I, er, called a few people, including the most senior hairdresser in town, and the rumor is..."

"What?"

"That Tom Rudden is in a relationship with Linda."

Chase raised an eyebrow. "Orson's wife?"

"They're separated, I was told," Kara said.

"Yes," Catherine said.

"I, er, didn't want to impugn your aunt's reputation with a rumor." Kara's flush deepened.

"It's okay. Tony and I were never very close to Linda. Orson married her a few years before Dad died so we were already young teens and we probably weren't the easiest age for family bonding. She didn't like us much, or that's the vibe we got anyway. I wondered if she resented our uncle for helping us get new identities and sending us money while we were in hiding."

"Maybe resented you enough that she and Tom Rudden would work out a plan to help Stone kidnap Orson?" Stephanie asked.

Chase twiddled his pencil. "Kind of an improbable theory. Stone would have had to contact Tom and Linda between the time he escaped capture in Durnsville and the moment he abducted Catherine at the coffee shop. Unless he'd planned his escape somehow and contacted Linda before he made that happen. Is there any direct connection between Rudden and Stone?"

"Not as far as I've heard," Kara said.

Chase laughed. "Your hairdresser knows everything."

Kara nodded. "Hairdressers hold the key to a lot of secrets, but rumors aren't always facts."

"See if you can verify with other sources, okay?" Garrett said.

Kara nodded.

The matter of the social security numbers nagged at him. He'd look into it, hopefully find out it wasn't what he feared, and he'd not involve Catherine unless he had to. But if her uncle had paid for stolen identities, and he didn't see how it could be otherwise, she'd have to know about it before too much longer.

In spite of the knot coiled in his gut, he waited as patiently as he could while Catherine attempted to get her aunt on the phone. "She's not answering her cell. It's the only number I have for her."

"Where does she live since she and Orson split up?"

"A condo in Silverton. I need to go there."

Steph, Chase and Garrett all shook their heads.

"I know it's not the greatest scenario, with Stone on the loose it's a bad idea, but I want to ask her personally about staying at the house." She paused. "More than that, I need to be sure she's okay. She and Uncle Orson might be on the outs, but she's still his wife and he'd want me to check on her."

Chase held up a finger. "I don't think Stone will try again in a suburban area like that, but how about I get you a police escort? Hagerty said they were sending someone out there to ask her a few questions so maybe we can combine errands." He didn't wait for Garrett to object. He wouldn't anyway. Catherine was clearly in danger and being under direct police supervision was the only thing that would calm him at the moment.

Chase set about contacting Hagerty. Catherine sat with Pinky and Kara did her best to keep her company. The sprinkling rain increased to torrents. It took an hour or so, but Chase finally announced he'd made contact.

"All set," he said.

Pinkerton was ecstatic to escape the confines of the house. Catherine scrubbed him behind the ears as Garrett attached a yellow raincoat around his stocky body.

"His Gorton fisherman look. He's not wild about it, but you don't want to smell a wet bloodhound, believe me."

"I hope he gets to stay inside during the storm."

"They all have outdoor kennels and a covered dog run but we're pretty loosey-goosey with the rules. Especially…" He trailed off.

"Especially what?"

"Well, Pinky doesn't like me to mention it but he's afraid of thunder."

She laughed, a long silvery musical sound that enveloped him with a strange stomach fluttering feeling, and kissed Pinkerton on the brow. "That makes two of us." She whispered, "Your secret is safe with me, Pinky."

Garrett thought the dog looked a little brighter. Pinky was beginning to take quite a shine to Catherine. Garrett could not dismiss what could only be described as a glow, having her close. That startled him so much he nearly tripped over Pinkerton's gangly legs as they walked to the garage to borrow Roman's car.

Yesterday he'd have said he never wanted to be in the same room with the woman who reminded him of his most profound failure. Today…he couldn't stand the thought that she'd be out of his reach.

Catherine glanced at him, pushing the bangs from her face. "You okay?"

"Me? Oh, sure. Tip-top. Why do you ask?"

"Because you're trying to unlock the car door with a can opener."

He looked at the gizmo in his palm. "Oh, duh. I was camping with Pinky last time I wore this jacket and we were roughing it. I don't mind sleeping outside and packing in meals and such, but I always forget the can opener for Pinky's food so I packed an extra."

She smiled. "I like camping too, but I never thought to pack an emergency can opener."

He tethered Pinky into the back seat, hoping his cheeks weren't red. *How about you try not to look like a fool for the next fifty miles? Easygoing, glib, the life of the party, remember? Not an eighth grade boy with a foot in his mouth.* At least he'd taken Catherine's mind off what happened the last time he'd driven her someplace.

Hagerty sent an officer and they met him at the security gate. The rain pounded in angry waves as they made the journey. The roar of it thankfully took away the need for small talk. She consulted her phone for directions. Linda's condo was in a newer development in Silverton, a byproduct of the influx of people fed up with the challenges of bigger cities. The boxy two-story structures were what his father would have termed "spiffy." He would also have recommended Garrett simply "pang-wangle" his way forward, or carry on in spite of whatever challenges cropped up. As a teen, he'd never wanted his friends to hear his father's wild "dad-isms." As an adult, he'd give everything he had to listen to his father one more time.

Considering the woman beside him had lost her father too, he should be working even harder to be sure she didn't lose her sister as well. He gripped the wheel, checked the rearview for the millionth time and took the last turn to arrive at the correct house number. The officer idled at the curb, talking on the radio.

In the driveaway, a short, sixtysomething woman was loading items from her trunk and stacking them inside the garage. Three damp cardboard boxes and a Tiffany lamp dripped water onto the cement floor. He heard Catherine gasp.

"That lamp's from my uncle's living room." Before he

could stop her, she'd exited the car. He hopped out and caught up, while Pinkerton slobbered on the window as he watched them.

Linda jerked a glance at Catherine. If she was surprised to see her there, it didn't show. Her dark hair, swept into a twist, was damp from raindrops, as was her navy windbreaker. She quickly shut her trunk and stepped out of the garage.

"Aunt Linda," Catherine said. "I've been trying to call."

She zipped her windbreaker. "I've been busy."

Catherine stood tall, unbowed by the rain. "I can see that. I, uh, wanted to be sure you'd heard about Uncle Orson."

"Yes."

The silence lingered too long. "Are those things from Uncle Orson's house? That lamp… It was my great grand-father's."

"Our house," she corrected. "We're husband and wife, at least on paper. He bought that place for me when we were married."

Garrett figured he'd try and calm the waters. "We're sorry about what happened to Orson."

She remained unsmiling. "I'm sure you didn't come here to express your concern, or to track what I'm taking from my own house."

The cop finally strolled over to join them. "Hello, ma'am," he said as he identified himself.

"What do you want?" she said coldly.

He continued, undeterred. "The chief asked if you might have any recent pictures of Orson."

"No," she said. "I don't."

He paused. "All right. We'd like to search the property again, with your permission. To be sure we didn't miss anything the first time."

"Feel free, but don't leave the place a mess."

"Yes, ma'am."

Tom Rudden opened the interior garage door, engrossed in reading from a paper, oblivious to the people gathered in the driveway. "Linda, we can get at least two thousand dollars for that Persian rug in the—"

"The one in my uncle's foyer?" Catherine said.

Rudden jerked and looked up. "I didn't know you were here."

"Obviously." Catherine appealed to the police officer. "Can they sell things from my uncle's home without his permission?"

The police officer looked decidedly uncomfortable. "We'd have to look into the legalities of that, but until the homeowner has been found…"

Linda waved a hand. "Stone kidnapped Orson to get to Antonia, isn't that right? Though I can't imagine why Stone would be so obsessed with that girl like that to risk coming back here."

Catherine flinched. "It's my sister you're talking about."

"Yes," she said coldly, "I know. She toyed with Stone, leading him to think she was interested, but I'm sure she was simply looking for a good time. A country kid like that would be way too simple for her tastes."

"Ma'am…" Garrett began, but Catherine cut him off.

"What is your problem with us exactly?" Anger brightened her eyes to indigo. "You've always disliked us and as far as I know, we never did anything to hurt you."

"Never did anything?" Linda snorted. "So you don't think siphoning off our assets is hurtful at all?"

Catherine and the cop looked equally puzzled. Garrett's expression no doubt matched theirs.

Linda pointed a manicured finger. "Look, sweetie. Your uncle may be unable to say no to you two, but I'm not. That house is still half mine, until the divorce is official, and I can take what I want, when I want, no matter what his precious nieces say."

The cop cleared his throat. "I suggest we end this meeting for now."

"We barely know you," Catherine said with a hitch in her voice that made Garrett draw closer to her.

"You are two spoiled, entitled women who cried sob stories to Orson to milk him dry."

"Mrs. Hart—" the cop interjected, but she interrupted him again.

"Johnson, I never took his name." Her narrowed gaze riveted on Catherine. "Yeah, you had something terrible happen to you when your dad was murdered, but you're grown adults and you shouldn't be mooching off of your uncle."

Catherine gaped. "I don't. I've supported myself since I was twenty. I don't know what you've been told but—"

"Right, right. Whatever. I'm divorcing Orson and then he can take all his share and give it to you both, for all I care. If he wants to bankrupt himself to keep you living the good life, so be it. His choice, but he's not giving away my money. I don't owe you two anything." Rudden nodded at her side.

"We'll go now." Garrett reached for Catherine's wrist.

"Why don't you do that?" Rudden said.

The cop tried to usher them down the driveway, but Catherine wasn't done.

She pointed to the garage. "Convenient that my uncle isn't here to stop you from taking what you want. Did you have anything to do with his abduction?"

Garrett schooled his face to hide the shock from Catherine's attack. The desperation rang clear in her words. She'd lit the match. He watched to see if the burning fuse would reveal anything.

The cop was observing carefully too.

Linda rolled her eyes. "I'm not some criminal master-mind. How would I do that?"

Since Linda was not likely to entertain a second conversation with them at a later date, Garrett decided to press. "You're involved with Mr. Rudden. Maybe he intentionally disabled the security system that day to give Stone easy access."

Her expression showed no surprise at his accusation, but the tiny tightening of her mouth indicated there was no doubt that she was romantically involved with Rudden.

"The system failed on its own," Rudden said darkly.

"I don't have to listen to this. Get off my property." Linda dashed through the rain, yanked open her car door and slid inside. Rudden got in the passenger seat and activated the garage door, which closed with a squeal. The engine roared and Pinkerton barked.

Before he could stop her, Catherine hurried to Linda's driver's side window, fear clear on her face. "Please. I don't want your money or your property. I just need my uncle back. If you know where he is…"

Linda flashed a look of pure rage at Catherine and gunned the motor. Garrett pulled her out of the way. Linda drove off, her tires clipping the cement curb and shaving off sprinkles of rubber.

Catherine stood immobile in the rain, resisting his efforts to move her to the car.

"I only want my uncle back." She melted into a sob.

The cop passed them and got into his squad car, then began talking on his cell phone from behind the wheel.

Garrett pulled her into his arms and squeezed her tight as if the pressure could press away her pain. "It's okay. We'll find him."

She cried into his shoulder and when he tucked his head near hers to shield her from the rain, he found his mouth in close proximity to hers. *Don't do it.* But he could not resist and he kissed her.

She leaned into him and returned the kiss. It was as if the raindrops cocooned them, folding them into a place where the pain and fear faded into warmth and comfort. Sparks danced through his nerves and he longed to kiss her again, but she looked down. When she once again buried her face into his chest, he rocked her back and forth for a moment before he propelled her into the vehicle. Behind the wheel, he turned on the heater, anxious to do something, anything, to keep from focusing on the fact that he'd just kissed her. And she'd kissed him back.

Pinkerton took the opportunity to swab the rain from Catherine's neck with his pink ribbon of a tongue. He was grateful to his dog for easing the awkwardness. Bloodhounds were never at a loss for what to do. Lick, sniff, follow, eat or sleep. That basically carried them through any situation.

"It'll be warm in a minute," he blurted, still fussing with the vents. "I'm sorry that didn't go well, you know, with your aunt."

Catherine gulped. "My dad had a small life insurance policy, and Tony and I got that plus proceeds from the house, which wasn't much. There were so many expenses with the funeral, paying off credit cards and the house needed a ton of work to make it sellable. After we left the area, Uncle Orson helped us out for several years, but as soon as I was on my feet I told him to keep his money."

"You don't have to explain."

"I don't want you to think…"

He took her hand. "I don't."

They watched the rain slam against the windshield, each lost in thought. Linda's hostility. Catherine's pain. That kiss…

"Can't believe I was concerned Aunt Linda might be worrying about Orson."

He was still trying to steady his emotions. *Get it together. What's the next move?* He wouldn't suggest again that she stay at the ranch more than one night. Not yet. It wasn't the moment, but it was clear that Linda wasn't the ally Catherine had hoped for. Would he go so far as to say she was an enemy? She definitely had reasons to be happy Orson was out of the way. Improbability aside, might she have formed an alliance with Stone to meet both their goals? She'd have access to the property. Stone would have Orson to lure Antonia. Rudden would get a share of Orson's assets and cement his loyalty to Linda by greasing the skids for the abduction.

His thoughts lurched a step further. And what if Linda arranged for Orson not to come back at all? For Stone to kill him once he had Antonia? Determined not to let suspicion get the better of him, he put the car in gear.

They followed the cop. At the exit to the subdivision, he caught a movement from the bluff above them, a small cascade of rocks sliding. His muscles tightened. From someone climbing there?

"Hunch down a minute, okay?"

Catherine obeyed as he kept moving and called the cop, who doubled back to take a look. Garrett directed him to the spot he'd noted.

The cop called on his cell. "Don't see anything. All clear."

Was it? Might it have been Stone tracking them?

The cop's tone indicated he didn't think so.

Catherine took her seat and they drove away from Linda's, the officer setting a quick pace.

A half mile later, Catherine startled him by speaking.

"She's taking things that mean something to my uncle and she doesn't care about the sentiment at all. It—it was more than I could stand." She heaved a deep breath. "I didn't handle the conversation right at all, did I?"

"What you lacked in finesse, you made up for with sincerity," he said, trying to coax her to smile. Before he could continue, she gulped in a breath and tears began to trickle down her face. Clearly that hadn't been the right thing to say. Pinky immediately stretched and applied his big nose to her ear.

She stroked Pinky's silky head until the dog eased back again.

Garrett tried to think of another joke, but his mouth decided on something completely different. "This is difficult stuff, Catherine, and you're doing your best."

She sighed. "My best just put Linda and Rudden on the offense, big-time. That wasn't smart."

"Give yourself a break. You're a work in progress without—"

"A completion date," she said, finishing his sentence.

He goggled. "How did you know I was going to stay that?"

She smiled and swiped at her tears. "You told me before."

"I did?"

"Yes. That time you came to our house to check on us a couple of days after my dad was killed."

Seventy-two hours after he'd lost Stone at the arraignment. The manhunt was in full force, he'd been working around the clock, desperate to recapture the killer who'd escaped due to his negligence.

"We went back there one last time to pack our stuff to move to my uncle's. I was flipping out, tearing my room apart, because I'd lost a paper I needed to turn in. I think I was kind of in shock still. We were about to move to Orson's, try to finish out high school. Remember?"

A mental image floated to the surface. "I remember you were upset. I don't recall doing much to help."

"You did. You calmed me down and helped me search until I found the paper. You asked if I was hungry and you ordered burgers for me and Tony. We ate outside, on the porch, even though it was raining."

He flashed back on that occasion, two sisters experiencing the worst moments of their lives. He'd been completely uncertain if he should even go, considering what had happened with Stone. But he'd not felt blame then, not from Catherine. She'd been too trusting and too grieving to understand what he'd allowed to happen. Antonia had refused to eat any of the fast food, or even sit in the same room with him. Antonia was the more perceptive of the two, her demeanor making him wonder if his presence was helping or making things worse. "I'm glad I did something nice."

"I never considered how much courage it took for you to show up then."

"Long on courage, short on common sense."

"I graduated high school before I moved away, but Antonia couldn't bear it. When she got that anonymous threat on her car windshield just before school ended her junior year, she knew it was from Stone. Maybe we should have gone to the cops then, but Uncle Orson said he'd handle it and he did. New identities and money to start fresh somewhere safe. Tony went to stay with a friend's family until she completed high school online. I wish we'd stayed closer, in spite of the risk." Catherine didn't smile as she turned to look at him, the gleam of tears luminous in the dim light. "Wonder why it's easier to remember the mistakes we make than the good things we've done?"

His throat thickened. "Yeah. Even though we know God forgives, why can't we really trust that enough to act like it?"

Her lower lip quivered and he swallowed.

"Yes," she whispered. "Even though." She was silent, gazing into the bleak sky. "Garrett, I want you to know I did blame you, for years, once I fully understood what had happened at the arraignment…but I don't anymore."

Tears pricked his eyes. The rain pattered down harder. "You don't?"

"No. This whole bizarre situation, meeting you again, it's…caused me to look at things differently. You did the best you could. And you're doing your best for us now."

He could hardly answer. Did he deserve her forgiveness? Would he have extended it if the situation was reversed? Yes, he thought, and his pleasure was immense. "Thank you," he mumbled. "For saying that."

She took a deep breath and let it out. "We're both works in progress."

He chuckled. "I'll take it."

She nodded and straightened in her seat. "Okay. What's next?"

The windshield wipers slashed at the downpour as the cop pulled off and let them drive past onto Security Hounds property.

"We'll situate you in Roman's trailer. You can get some rest. Maybe Pinky can keep you company in case there's any thunder?"

At the mention of his name, Pinky thumped his tail against the seat.

She smiled. "Okay. Pinky and I will weather the storm and you can go to the hospital and check on your mother."

How had she known that's what he was thinking? But

Catherine seemed to know what he needed more than he did. She'd forgiven him.

The rage of the storm increased as he drove.

His bubble of happiness popped when he considered that Catherine's life would be at risk until Stone was caught.

They'd find Antonia or Stone, or both. And Orson too.

And then the Hart family would have their lives back.

After that, he could sort out the wild emotions thumping through him since their kiss.

Catherine's phone buzzed and she glanced at the screen. He saw her jaw tense, mouth tighten.

"What is it?"

She was silent for a beat. "Nothing important."

"Really?"

"Yes." Her tone was light, airy.

And now he had another question on his mind.

Why was Catherine lying to him?

NINE

Catherine locked herself in the bathroom in the ranch house and checked her screen again with trembling hands, rereading the text.

Need help. Don't bring Garrett. I'm at the gate to the ranch.

Her pulse pounded. Of course, it could be the perfect trap. Stone might have gotten Antonia's phone somehow and he was luring Catherine out there to abduct her. There was no way she was going to hand herself over like a lamb to slaughter. But if she was wrong? If it really was Antonia texting?

While she tried to figure out what to do, the phone vibrated with a call. She answered.

"Can you talk? Are you alone?" It was indeed her sister's voice.

The breath rushed out and her body sagged in relief. "Yes. I'm alone. What's going on? Are you really at the gate?"

"Yes, but I don't have time to explain. Do you have any money? A warm jacket?"

"Tony…"

"Bring them to me, okay? Now. Can you get away without being seen?"

"I'm not going to do that. This is ridiculous. I know you

think you can handle Stone by yourself, but you can't. He killed our father, remember? He's got Uncle Orson imprisoned somewhere. This is a dangerous man and we need help."

"Other people will only make things worse. Stone will kill our uncle if he gets a whiff of cops or PIs, especially Garrett Wolfe." Her tone was venomous.

"Tony, please be smart about this. You are not some sort of vigilante—"

"Catherine," she snapped, then quieted with a loud exhale. "You promised you'd take care of me after Dad…" There was a soft, small gulp. "I need you to keep your promise right now. Nobody else, just you. I'm at the gate. Please come." And then she disconnected.

Catherine stared at the phone. Emotional manipulation aside, she had promised to take care of Tony. And she would. But this harebrained scheme of her sister's must be brought to a speedy close. The only way she was going to talk Tony out of her mission was a face-to-face encounter. If Tony saw Garrett, she might not cooperate, or worse yet, she'd bolt.

The choice was clear. She'd tell Garrett where she was going, it would be foolish not to, but insist on meeting Antonia herself. Garrett could stand by in the house in case she needed him, or even watch through binoculars.

Decision made, she marched from the bathroom.

Garrett was huddled around the phone with his siblings. "Sorry," he whispered. "Hospital conference call about Mom."

His mouth was pinched with concern.

Her plan crumbled on the spot. There was no way she'd interrupt that important conversation. New plan. She'd handle the Antonia meeting without troubling them and hopefully return with her stubborn sister in tow. She nodded to Garrett and pointed outside. When the door closed softly behind her, she hurried down the steps and along the path that led to the trailer. Hopefully Garrett was too engrossed in the phone call to look out the kitchen window and abandon his call to stop her. She jogged by her temporary residence and scurried into the tree-shrouded section that led downhill to the security gate.

The crowded canopy of branches kept off most of the rain, but not the chill. She pulled her coat tighter. Her sister wanted a jacket and money, huh? There was a wadded twenty in her pocket but she didn't intend to hand it over. Antonia was going to listen to reason if Catherine had to sit on her and holler in her ear. There would be no negotiation.

The metal gate came into view, a sturdy structure that blocked the road to any vehicles. It was more of a deterrent than a barrier since anyone on foot could hike onto the sprawling Security Hounds property.

The woods were still, except for the hum of the rain. She snuck a look backward. The ranch was far out of reach now, as was any chance Garrett would come to her aid if something happened. She squared her shoulders.

You don't need help. This is your sister and your problem.

"Tony?" she called. "Are you here?"

The wind scuttled leaves across her path as she peered into the foliage. "Tony?" she called again.

Antonia stepped from behind a screen of bushes, hair wild.

They embraced in a fierce hug. Tears splashed down Catherine's cheeks as she thanked God her sister was safe. Antonia shivered. Catherine immediately stripped off her jacket and wrapped it around her sister. "Don't get the idea I'm on board with your plan. We're going to walk back to the house and call the police."

"No, we aren't," Antonia said in her ear.

Catherine brought Antonia to arm's length and squeezed her wrists. "Honey, listen to me, please. I appreciate what you want to do. Daddy never got justice and it's not fair that

Porter Stone has made our lives a living nightmare, but I'm not going to watch you get yourself killed trying to punish him on your own. We're going to let the police—"

Antonia shook her off. "No, sis. That's not how to end this." Her eyes glittered like shards of ice.

Where had her quirky, effervescent sibling gone? The woman standing before her was deeply wounded, rigid with determination and anger. Catherine grieved the loss of innocence they'd both experienced at the hands of Porter Stone. "I'm sorry, Tony. We've got to do this the right way."

Her lips thinned and she glared at Catherine. "You don't understand."

"I do. It was my father too, remember? My uncle's missing. I'm just as worried as you are."

Antonia unzipped the jacket pocket and extracted the twenty-dollar bill with a grin. "You always keep cash in your pockets for an emergency. Well, this definitely qualifies."

"That's not why—"

A bird shot from an overhead branch, startling them both.

Antonia moved away a step. "I have to go. The longer I stay here, the greater chance he's followed me and you're in danger too."

"Exactly. We need to…"

A branch snapped and Catherine twisted around. As if out of a dream, Stone appeared behind Catherine, with a sly smile.

He locked eyes on Antonia. "You always thought you were smarter than me didn't you, Tony?"

Catherine immediately stepped between Stone and her sister. "Get away from us."

He pulled something from his pocket—the knife. He was armed and so much stronger than they were. Could she physically prevent him from taking Antonia?

"Tony, run to the house. Get help," she muttered to her sister. She felt Antonia moving closer instead of following her command.

"Listen to me, Porter," Tony snapped. "This is between me and you. It has nothing to do with my sister."

"Agreed. I don't want Catherine. I only needed her to get to you."

Tony shifted. "Then let her leave and you can have me. I'll go with you right now."

"No," Catherine snapped. "That is not happening. You'll have to go through us both and I think you'll regret it."

He laughed. "The Hart sisters. Small but mighty."

"That's right. And you're going to find out how mighty." Catherine's stomach was balled into a knot but she forced strength into her voice.

He raised the knife and stepped closer. "Get out of the way, Catherine."

Catherine tensed, arms up, ready to take him off his feet if she could.

From the direction of the ranch house, she heard a howl, then another.

"They're coming," Catherine said, feeling a gleam of hope. Help was on the way.

Stone shifted uneasily as the sound of running paws and feet carried through the air.

"If they catch you, you'll be arrested. The cops won't believe you," Antonia growled at Stone. "No one will."

Catherine willed her sister to stay quiet. Antagonizing the man wasn't going to buy them the precious moments they needed.

The barking turned into a noisy cacophony. Two blood-hounds, Chloe and Pinkerton, barreled over the ground with

Dana Mentink 109

Garrett and Steph right behind them. Chase was a minute behind them with Tank.

"I'll never leave you or Catherine alone," Stone said edging back toward the bushes. "Not until you pay, Antonia. She'll never be free of me and neither will you. You won't get your uncle back. I'll kill him and it will be your fault."

Antonia moved to run to him, but Catherine grabbed her by the arms.

She struggled. "Let me go, Cath. You don't understand." She clung with all her might.

"Catherine," Antonia screamed, thrashing now.

Stone turned to run.

A moment before he vanished, Antonia shouted, "I'll meet you at our place in Burney, Porter. I'll call you and tell you when I'll be there. We'll settle it once and for all."

Our place?

Stone's eyes narrowed. He nodded once, whirled around and plunged away into the trees.

Catherine held on but her sister hauled herself free except for one wrist. "You're not leaving. Whatever you're planning, stop it right now."

Antonia smiled, jerked her other wrist free. "Sorry, sis. Thanks for the jacket." She snagged a foot out and caught Catherine's ankle, bringing her to the ground.

Catherine tumbled backward but she was up again in a moment, head spinning, looking around wildly.

The dogs overtook her, a slobbering, tail-wagging mob as Steph and Chase pursued Stone, Garrett stopping by her side.

Stone was gone.

And so was Antonia.

Garrett bandaged the scrape on Catherine's elbow. He felt the tension still humming through her body. Chase had gone back to the house to alert Hagerty, but he didn't have much hope. Stone had a vehicle hidden somewhere; he had no doubt. Maybe the SUV he'd stolen from Orson's or something else he'd swiped. There was no use risking the safety of the dogs to track Antonia at the moment either.

"You…" He was going to berate Catherine for setting off on her own to meet her sister, putting herself at enormous risk, but the words died away. He silently thanked God he'd seen her hurrying off so he'd ended the phone conference and they'd pursued.

When they got back to the house, Chase had hung up with the police and Stephanie was on hold with the hospital to try and reschedule and reassure their mother, who was likely climbing the walls.

Catherine thanked him, her voice a monotone. "I was going to convince her to stop running."

"You said she told Stone she'd meet him at their place in Burney. What did she mean by that?"

Catherine was still shivering. He snagged a soft blanket and draped it across her shoulders.

"I was trying to remember. They only dated for…" Catherine stopped. "Wait a minute. She told me that on their second date he took her to Burney Falls. They hiked to some cabin owned by a friend of his, but I don't know the exact location."

Garrett pulled a map from the shelf and spread it on the table. "This is Whisper Valley and surrounds. Burney's a big area and she's on foot. How would she get there?"

Catherine groaned. "My sister is resourceful. She'll hitchhike, maybe. And Stone probably still has the SUV. But what about my uncle? Do you think… I mean, wouldn't it be risky to move him from here to Burney? Unless he's…"

Garrett squeezed her shoulder. "We can't think that way. Until we know differently, we'll assume your uncle is okay."

Chase filled bowls for Tank, Chloe and Pinkerton. The dogs set to work slopping water everywhere.

"We should strongly consider Catherine's theory about Burney," Garrett said.

"I admire her spirit, but it's rugged there," Chase said. "That'd be no easy hike to a cabin."

Catherine nodded. "My sister has completed a lot of training, survival stuff. She told me she did one of those experiences where they drop you in the wilderness for three days with minimal supplies and you have to find your way out."

"Oh, boy." Chase drained a bottle of water. "And Stone has a vehicle, but it won't be easy to transport Orson there. He's familiar with the area though, so he might know a way. Spent a lot of time climbing and such, didn't he?"

"Yes." Garrett toyed with his napkin. That was the Porter Stone he'd known, or thought he did. Someone who loved to be outside. Happy, easygoing, content.

Until he wasn't.

Until Antonia broke up with him and his affection turned to obsession. And when Catherine's father had argued with him...

"Burney Falls is in Shasta County." Chase glanced at the rain, which was now splattering the window. "About an hour and forty-five minutes driving time from here."

Steph hung up the phone. "Conference call rescheduled two hours from now." She looked at the map.

Garrett knew his twin was thinking about the hazards. The water that fed the falls came from underground springs, which provided an explosive flow rate of 379 million liters per day, even during the dry summer months. Snowmelt was at its peak now.

"We tracked a missing camper there when the park rangers needed assistance," Steph said.

"There's a reason Teddy Roosevelt called it the Eighth Wonder of the World." Kara jotted notes on her iPad.

At the moment, it felt anything but wondrous to think that Antonia might be heading for the state park. All that water... an icy forty-two degrees year-round.

"I'll ask Hagerty to alert the rangers to be on the lookout for either Antonia or Stone," Stephanie said, poking at her phone. "But the weather's horrible."

Steph drew several circles with a compass. "I'm suggesting we break up into two teams."

Steph glanced out the window. "I hate to be a Debbie Downer here, but this storm's going to hit full force this evening and we need to prep supplies."

Catherine groaned. "Please don't tell me we can't start the search until tomorrow."

"It would be unsafe for us and the dogs," Garrett said gently. "Tomorrow we'll have a morning window. Leave before sunup."

She pulled in a deep breath. "Before sunup. I guess I'll have to accept that."

Garrett shifted a little on his chair. "I've been wanting to ask about another topic, the identities for you and your sister."

"What about them?"

"Your uncle provided you with new ones? How exactly?"

She frowned. "He gave us names, money to get started elsewhere."

Chase cocked his chin at her. "Are you still using the same social security number you had as Catherine Hart?"

"No, Uncle Orson thought it would be too easy to track us so he got us new ones."

The air in the room seemed to grow heavy as they all looked at her.

"Where did he get them?" Garrett asked softly.

"I never asked." She pushed away her coffee. "But if you're saying he did something wrong…"

Garrett held up his hands. "I didn't mean to upset you."

"It does upset me that you're implying he could have broken the law. Bad enough he's been kidnapped." Her tears bubbled close to the surface and she got to her feet. Pinkerton bustled over to lick her wrist. "And why is that relevant anyway, Garrett? I thought we were focused on finding my sister and my uncle. If that's not your priority, I don't want your help."

"It is the priority." He gestured for her to sit in the chair. When she didn't, he sighed. "Please."

She hesitated, trailing her fingers over Pinkerton's furrowed brow. "I actually did wonder where he had gotten our new social security numbers, but I guess I never really wanted to know. Uncle Orson was the closest thing we had to a father." Slowly, she settled back into her chair.

"We'll leave that issue for the moment," Chase said.

But it wouldn't surprise Garrett if Kara's flying fingers didn't clear up the mystery of the social security numbers before long. He tried to breathe away the concern. *Priorities, remember?*

Catherine rubbed her temples. "I should go. Stay at Uncle Orson's. Maybe Tony will come there for supplies or something."

"I don't think that's a good idea."

Catherine swallowed, looking as if she was doubting her decision, doubting everything. Was she doing the right thing insisting on staying there? Would she ever find a safe place in this world? He had a desperate craving to show her that all was right and she was cared for, secure. Garrett covered her hand with his.

"You're not alone," he said. "Not anymore."

He heard her tiny gulp. Pinky curled out his tongue and gave her another warm slurp. A rumble of thunder ripped through the clouds.

She pulled in a breath. "What do we do next?"

"We make a war plan. Assign the search grids around the areas with cabins, gather our supplies, hit the ground running tomorrow and find your sister before she gets herself hurt."

"That plan sounds good," she said. "And I'm going to help."

Garrett sighed. "Yep. I wasn't even going to suggest that you stay here. Burney is a huge area to cover, but if Antonia is there, Pinkerton will find her."

"Or Chloe," Steph said.

"Or Tank," Chase added.

Steph gathered up the map. "One of us needs to stay at the hospital with Mom. It took hammer and tongs to get her to agree to let one of us be there. It's possible they'll do her surgery tonight if an opportunity presents itself."

"I'll do it," Kara said. "Since I don't have a dog at the moment. I'll head over first thing in the morning. I'll keep you all posted and if anything goes sideways, we can recalculate."

Chase gave her a thumbs-up. "Okay, so I'll take Steph and the eastern grid. You've got Catherine and the western."

Steph rolled her eyes. "Why does it sound like we're in junior high picking kickball teams?"

Chase caught Garrett's eye. "It's rough terrain up there. Be sure…"

Steph raised a finger. "If you say to protect the women, I will have to express my displeasure."

"Well, we can't have that now, can we?" Chase joked. "I

was merely going to say that we'd best step lively because the storm will foul the conditions and I happen to know that Pinkerton, the tender sprout, doesn't like to get muddy. Neither does Chloe."

"Unlike Tank, who detests being clean." Steph rose from the table. "But point well taken. It's rough terrain and we've possibly got a killer in the area so radios charged and extra batteries, first-aid kits, the works." Her phone rang.

"Hello, Officer Hagerty," she said, putting it on speaker. "Perfect timing." She filled him in on their search plans.

He cleared his throat. "All right. You all know how to handle yourselves on a search and rescue mission, but remember you have the park rangers to back you up. Matter of fact, I've been on the horn with them about Stone so I'll let them know you're coming at first light. Something else you should know about before you dive in. We finished our analysis at Orson's house. Prints in the garage area belong to Stone, which isn't a surprise." He paused. "Housekeeper called to tell me there was something missing from the property besides the car. The security camera is still offline, so it's impossible to know if it was taken during the abduction or after."

"What?" Catherine demanded. "What's missing?"

"A gun, from the desk drawer, a Glock nineteen. The housekeeper confirms it was there when she put away his papers Tuesday morning."

Catherine's hands clenched into fists. "Stone took it."

"That was my first guess too, but none of his prints are in the study."

Catherine bit her lip. "He might have worn gloves?"

"Why for the study and not in the garage?" Kara said. "And how would Stone have known to look for it in the desk drawer? He'd never been to Orson's house before, according to the same housekeeper. Possible Linda or Tom might have told him where it was if they are somehow in league together, but it'd be just as easy for them to give it to him rather than him risking a break-in."

Garrett leaned back in his chair. "Did you have a cop stationed at the house?"

"Not since yesterday evening. Sorry, but we don't have the manpower to babysit a crime scene, especially after it's released."

"Antonia has a key to my uncle's house. I do too. Aunt Linda didn't want us to, but he sent them anyway."

The rain lashed against the roof.

"Does Antonia know how to shoot?" Chase said.

"Yes," she said finally, "Dad taught us, but she never had the patience to be good at it. Dad called her…"

"What?" Garrett asked.

Catherine took a breath. "Trigger, because he said she was likely to shoot first and think it over later."

The silence was so profound Garrett could hear the grandfather clock ticking from the entry. He checked his watch. "Maybe she snuck into Orson's after she left the hospital? Stowed it somewhere when she came here to meet Catherine?"

"Yep," Chase said. "Plenty of possibilities."

Garrett felt as though the storm outside was battering the walls, trying to get in.

"If Tony's armed…" Catherine said.

"Then we better make sure we find her, or Stone, first."

If they didn't…someone wasn't going to come out of it alive.

He looked at Catherine's pained expression.

Her sister's life hung in the balance.

Please let us get there in time.

TEN

Catherine watched Garrett make dinner preparations in the cheerful kitchen. She snuggled down on the sofa cushions with Pinkerton.

She'd attempted to protest. She didn't want him fussing, but it felt so good to be taken care of. Because the attention was from Garrett? Yes, and what's more it was balm to her soul to have expressed her forgiveness. Mind-boggling. Unexpected, but true. She could breathe a little deeper, rest more soundly, move about her world with a weight removed.

Antonia would probably never come around to her way of thinking, but her sister hadn't had the opportunity to know Garrett in a deeper way. To her, he was the cop that let Stone escape…but he was so much more than that, Catherine realized.

She fingered her lips, the warmth of his earlier kiss still lingering there. What had that meant to him? What did it mean to her? Comfort? Friendship? Something more? She considered how it would feel to spend the night on the Security Hounds property. Beyond the wraparound porch, the fenced front yard was quiet, the dogs having taken shelter in the house or outdoor run. Kara was preparing for her turn at the hospital and Stephanie was likely prepping supplies and researching on her computer.

Were they ferreting out the truth of her social security number? Pinkerton lolled next to her, draping himself across her lap for better tummy-scratching access. She obliged, lost in thought. Until the Wolfes had brought up the topic, she'd refused to think about how her uncle had supplied her and Tony with new identities. She wasn't naive, she'd simply never allowed herself to go there. Why?

Because you didn't want to consider that he might have done something illegal. It was not blind naivety, as her sister might have accused her of. It was the fact that Orson and Tony were all she had and she couldn't bear to acknowledge any serious flaws. Was that wrong?

She didn't know. Still, she was determined to trust in Orson's innocence until facts proved otherwise.

She'd sent dozens of texts to Antonia since she'd bolted, pleading for a response, but she'd only succeeded in whiling away an hour and a half. Restless, she eased from under the snoring bloodhound and perused the family photos on the mantel. It was a few minutes before five o'clock. What was she supposed to do for the rest of the evening to keep from obsessing about her sister and uncle? Were they exposed to the elements? Scared?

Garrett snatched at his phone and listened attentively to the speaker before he disconnected.

Stephanie hustled down the hall and cornered her brother. "I heard your phone ring. Was it the hospital? Spill it."

Garrett nodded. "Surgery was moved up and they started prepping her. She didn't react well to some of the anesthesia."

Stephanie's expression turned stark and she grabbed her keys. "I'll go right now."

Garrett held her arm. "No. Wait. She's stable. Resting comfortably. Chase is there until midnight. He said to get some sleep, give him time to hear from the doctor and you can switch places with him in a couple of hours. Kara can take over after that since we'll be on the search."

"Has Chase actually laid eyes on her?"

"Yes, and that almost got him kicked out."

She sighed. "He's skirting the rules again?"

"More like hurtling over them as is typical for our big brother. Anyway he said he's staying put until you show up, and we should keep the home fires burning."

"So that means he's not at DEFCON-one level of concern."

Garrett nodded. "More like hovering around a four."

Catherine smiled at the sibling exchange.

Stephanie blew out a slow breath that seemed to come from her toes. "I hate waiting."

Garrett's gentle demeanor was back in place. "I know. That's why you always lose at checkers."

"Someday, I'll beat you," Stephanie said over her shoulder as she strode out.

"Uh-huh, and someday Chase will take up cake baking."

"You never know."

He smiled in that roguish way of his that made Catherine want to smile too. He looked over at her. "Dinner has been acquired. Ready to slog our way to the trailer?"

She agreed and they ran through the curtain of raindrops. The unit was spare but comfortable, a full-size bed at one end and a tidy kitchenette at the other, with a seating area sandwiched between them.

He poured glasses of water, rustled about in the bag of supplies and declined her offer to help. His movements were restless. She checked the time on her phone and groaned.

"Champing to get to your sister?"

"Yes." She tried not to picture Antonia out in the storm, with a gun, hurtling toward a deadly rendezvous with Stone. "It's such a long time until morning."

His stomach growled. "And a long time since my weeds-and-seeds muffin. Hungry?"

"As a matter of fact, yes."

Garrett brightened. "Excellent. Take a look at what I filched from the main kitchen." He pulled the items from his bag. "Kara must be worrying. She cooks when she's agitated, which works well for her hungry siblings. She's got a greenhouse Roman built her in the back, which Chase is forbidden to set foot in since he killed her plants by leaving the door open. You would not believe what she harvests in there. Tomatoes, peppers, onions and herbs." He snagged a container. "There's fresh salsa and…" He produced a foil package. "Homemade tortillas in here. How about some dinner? I can manage to make a quesadilla with this stuff if your standards aren't too exacting."

"Sounds perfect to me." She could not remember the last time someone had cooked for her. Even on her sporadic meetings with Antonia and Orson, she was always the one to prepare the meals. It was pleasant to watch Garrett bustle around. He seemed happier, she thought, though the tension in his shoulders remained.

The smell of browning tortillas and melting cheese made her mouth water. She'd just set paper napkins on the table when the wind began to lash rain against the roof. A rumble of thunder sounded and Pinkerton leaped to his feet, shivering.

"It's okay, sweetie," Catherine said, hastening to rub his ears.

"On second thought, the storm's going to sound pretty loud out here." He arched an eyebrow at her. "Sure you can't be persuaded to bunk in the house tonight?"

"The trailer is fine, really. It's secure, right?"

"Well, I can see you from my room and the security gate

will be locked…but after the latest Stone episode it'd be safer if you'd allow me to sleep on the trailer sofa. He probably won't be back, but we can't be sure."

His tone was casual and calm, but there were two spots of color on his cheeks, which probably matched her own.

He was committed enough to her protection to inconvenience himself that much? Of course he was. He'd risked his life for her, hadn't he? He was juggling his beloved mother's care to enact a plan to save her sister. Too much, too soon, for a man she'd believed to be the source of her family's pain. And trusting anyone, especially a man, especially an extremely handsome man, was something at which she was rusty indeed.

"No," she blurted, dropping a napkin and hastily retrieving it. "There's no need. The gate's locked and if Stone truly is in Burney waiting for Antonia, he's hours from here."

Garrett regarded his dog. "Pinky snores loud but he'd bark fit to be tied if he heard an intruder. How about if he's your security agent tonight and I just keep him company for a few hours? I have some work to do on my phone anyway."

Pinkerton flopped an ear in their direction at the mention of his name. Catherine giggled. "I don't think he likes you mentioning his snoring…but offer accepted."

"Super."

At the table, he startled her by reaching for her hand when they said grace. He added a plea for God to watch over Antonia, Orson and his mother, then they dug in. The words made her tear up. For so long she'd felt like she was the only person in the universe praying for Antonia and Orson, since neither were believers. Now there was someone else.

"These are delicious," Catherine said, after a bite of cheesy tortilla.

He added sour cream and salsa to his. "That's because

my sister's salsa is the bomb. She makes a version without cilantro just for me."

They munched while Pinkerton ate from his bowl, stopping every few moments to listen for thunder.

Garrett stared out the window.

"You're worried about your mother, aren't you?" she said.

"Yes. And you, your sister and uncle. Plenty of concern floating around."

"I try not to waste time worrying, but it's a battle. Dad used to tell me worry is making plans without God, but some circumstances I can't seem to help it."

His eyebrows arched. "Right? 'Battle' is the right word, for sure. When my dad was dying, I was on my knees plenty, praying that God would spare him and worrying the rest of the time."

And he'd been a young teen, close to the age she had been when her father was murdered. She remembered the hours after her father had been taken by the medics. She'd wailed to God to let it be a mistake, that there was some life left in her father that the medics hadn't detected. The sensation of anger and betrayal had dulled, but not completely died away. "And how did you feel when He didn't? Save your dad, I mean?"

He sat back and cocked his head at her. "For the first time in my life I felt angry at God. Enraged is more like it. He felt distant, indifferent, like my prayers were snippets tossed up into the air and blasted away by the wind, like I'd wasted my energy on a God that didn't care."

She'd felt exactly that way. Blasted and withered and alone. Her father, the faithful churchgoer who had raised his daughters to believe, was suddenly gone, ripped away. She'd lost him and she felt like she'd lost God too for a very long time.

A leaf slapped against the window, and they watched it

quiver and slide until it blew away. "But you don't feel like that now?" she said.

"Not anymore."

"Why?"

"My dad said something before he passed that changed my mind. Took me a while to remember it but I finally did."

She waited silently for him to continue. Her heart had been so stony until she encountered Garrett again. Before she would have doubted anything he said could penetrate, but their moments of connection had weakened her armor. "What changed for you?"

"Dad said, 'God's not your personal assistant, Garrett.'"

She blinked. Not what she'd expected. "What does that mean?"

"That's exactly what I asked him."

Pinkerton's snores from the sofa were a rumbly undertone.

Garrett continued. "It means we're meant to serve and worship Him because He's holy, not because He does or doesn't do what we want Him to."

"That makes God sound so cold, that He can allow cruelty and pain and loss and not care."

"He does care, but He's not there to do our bidding or solve all our problems."

An old scab ripped open inside her, the anger of a deeply wounded teen, fresh as it was all those years ago. "I didn't ask for much, Garrett. I prayed for my family, like you did. He let my dad get murdered anyway. Dad was a good man, a faithful follower. He didn't deserve what he got." Her skin rippled in goose bumps. Why had they started down this line of conversation when she'd thought she'd made an uneasy peace for herself?

Slowly he lifted his hand and covered hers. "I understand. Believe me. My dad was a good man too. Faithful, sincere. But if we only worshipped a God that gave us what we wanted, He'd be a cosmic vending machine, wouldn't He? A glorified personal assistant."

There was such tenderness on his face, a sincerity he mostly covered with wit and one-liners. He shook his head. "That's what my dad was trying to show me. God is worthy of my devotion, not because He answers my prayers the way I want Him to, but because He's God. He loves me, all of us, and He made us to love Him back, no matter what."

She let the words fall on her like the mist from the river. *Worthy because He's God, not because He gives me what I want.* It was as if her hazy thoughts, half-formed notions about God, were suddenly brought into a tangible shape, something bright and solid and lasting. So beautiful. So simple.

Tears filled her eyes as the memory came rushing back. She looked at her lap to hide her emotions, but she felt the pressure of his hand on hers, the touch communicating a question.

"I'd forgotten," she whispered.

"Forgotten what?"

She steadied herself with a deep breath. "I was young when my mother died, but I talked to Dad about it later when I was in high school. I asked him if he prayed that she'd be saved. He said he had. I asked how Dad could love God when He'd not kept her alive." She swallowed hard, forcing the words through her thick throat. "He said, 'We're not here just to receive. We're here to love, whatever that looks like.'"

"A wise father, like mine," Garrett said. "They'd have gotten along splendidly."

"I wish I'd understood it sooner."

"Me too." He shrugged and tapped his temple. "In my case, I had to clear out some of the wet noodles up there in my skull first."

"Garrett, can I ask you something?"

"Fire away."

She let the question fly, without filtering it. "Why do you pretend so much?"

He frowned. "Pretend?"

"Pretend you're always happy and glib."

"Not pretending." He winked. "Maybe I am always happy and glib."

She did not let him look away or defuse the moment with his joke. "Are you sure you aren't hiding behind the Mr. Charming thing?"

He shoved a hand through his dark hair. "Uh, well, someone has to be Mr. Charming, so it might as well be me."

"Right there. That's exactly what I'm talking about. When the conversation gets serious, when it comes down to sharing hard things, most of the time you crack jokes and make everyone laugh. This is the first time I've really had a deep conversation with you."

He opened his mouth, then closed it again. She regretted her boldness. *Calling him out, Catherine? Really? As if you two have that level of depth in your relationship?*

But he sat back and sighed. "I learned at an early age to cover up for my deficits with a joke. People liked me because I made them laugh, teachers and the other kids. Later, my fellow cops, my family."

She stayed quiet, silently coaxing him to go on.

He cleared his throat. "Uh, the laughter bought me time to come up with answers too, if I'm being totally honest. Dyslexia made me a tic slower to respond in school so the laugh track covered that up. I guess it was easier, less embarrassing."

"Less authentic," she said, surprised at his revelation.

His brow furrowed. "You're right. It was a great coping

mechanism, but it's also become a crutch. I never looked at it that way. Never had anyone call me on the carpet for it before, except maybe Steph."

"You're wonderfully funny." She interlaced his fingers with hers, squeezing. "And I do like Mr. Charming, but I like this Garrett very much too." *Like? Very much?* But nothing more was on the table with Garrett Wolfe. Was it? Even this deeper, more sincere side of him?

He might have blushed, but she wasn't certain. He pulled her hand to his lips and kissed her knuckles. "Thank you. It takes guts to tell someone the truth."

"You're welcome." She smiled back. "So God's not my personal assistant, and you're not my appointed court jester." She reoriented their joined hands into a shake. "Agreed?"

He shook, voice brimming with warmth. "Agreed, Catherine."

Why did the sound of him speaking her name warm her insides?

They finished their dinner, the moments stretching light and airy between them. It was the simplest of dinners, the humblest of surroundings, but she couldn't remember a time she'd enjoyed more.

As they cleaned up the leftovers, her phone buzzed. Unknown number, but something in her gut told her who was on the other end.

Her happiness drained away. A bolt of fear slammed her as she tapped the speakerphone button.

"Hello?"

"Why isn't she here yet?"

Her heart whacked into her ribs as Garrett moved to her side. "Who is this?"

"You know who it is," he shouted. "I want Antonia. She said she'd call and I've heard nothing."

"Where are you exactly?"

He hesitated. "She knows where. You don't need to. Did you convince her not to come?"

"Why?" Catherine said with a flash of anger. "Are you afraid of my sister? You think she's going to get the drop on you?"

"Shut up," he said. "I can handle Antonia better than you can. Did you convince her not to meet me?"

"I want to talk to my uncle."

"I asked you a question."

"And I'll answer it, after I talk to my uncle." Garrett squeezed her hand and she clutched his in return. Was her uncle still alive?

She heard the sound of movement. A familiar voice came on the line.

"Catherine?" he croaked.

"Uncle Orson." Her whole body prickled with elation. He was alive. Stone hadn't killed him. "I'm here. Are you hurt? Where's he keeping you?"

There was a grunt and Stone was back on the line.

"All right. Where's Antonia? Why hasn't she called?"

"We know where you are," Catherine said, choking back tears. "You're at the cabin in Burney, aren't you?"

"Answer my question," Stone roared.

"The police are on their way to arrest you right now."

"Yeah? Burney's a big, wild place. Searching for me will be like the needle in the haystack and no one's gonna risk it in the dark. I'll be gone in plenty of time anyway, just as soon as your sister shows up. So is she on her way?" The sound of his breathing filled the line. "Or do I kill your uncle?"

Catherine's terror ballooned and she could not utter a single syllable.

"Antonia's coming," Garrett said into the phone, "but you're not going to get out of this. We will find you before she does. You're trapped."

"I don't think so. And if I see any sign of a cop or a dog or one of your clan, I'm killing the old man. Think about it, Garrett. You had your chance to get me and you lost, now it's my turn." The line went dead.

"We can't wait," Catherine sobbed. "Please, Garrett. Please. We have to go to Burney now."

He eased her onto a chair and stroked her back. "We'll be there by sunrise, but we can't search in the dark. Your sister isn't going to be able to get very far until daylight either. She likely hasn't even made it to Burney yet. Stone's not going to kill your uncle until he's sure he has what he wants."

She was crying now, sobs shaking her body.

"What if we're too late for my sister and my uncle?" she whispered.

He folded her in his arms, squeezed her tight and prayed.

ELEVEN

Garrett's alarm buzzed at 4:00 a.m. From his perch on the trailer sofa, he'd heard Catherine tossing and turning for most of the night. Stone's call had unsettled him and terrified her. Antonia and Stone were both reckless and desperate, a lethal combination.

Garrett could feel the urgency rattling his nerves as he returned to the main house. Pinkerton was already keeping unusually close to Garrett, as if he could sense a mission on the horizon. He found Steph at the coffee maker.

"Did…?" Garrett didn't get the question out before Steph answered.

"Wally's in the outdoor kennel with a cushy blanket and seventeen chew toys. Matter of time before he digs out and we have to wrestle him from a mud hole."

She waved to the organized packs on the table. She'd have filled them with food, water, radios and first-aid kits. There was never a reason to hike in the mountains without the proper supplies. Their bloodhounds' sole responsibility was sniffing. All other survival details had to be considered and planned for by the humans.

Garrett flashed on the last case they'd worked, a lost camper near Burney Falls who'd failed to return to his group and whom the park service had been unable to locate. It hadn't ended well. The camper had slipped on some mossy rocks and tumbled into the river. He recalled that Pinkerton had gotten within ten feet of the victim, whose body was wedged between two rocks, and let out a mournful howl that stopped Garrett in his tracks and chilled him to the core.

Pinkerton knew before he did that they were engaged in a recovery not a rescue.

Was Antonia savvy enough to avoid the natural hazards as well as Stone's ill will? How would Catherine go on if her sister wound up like the camper? *Lord, please let this be a rescue...*

Before he hurried back to the trailer, he checked for messages.

One from the police replying to him about Stone's call and the search.

NPS is alerted. Radio your search coordinates to them when you're in the park. And he imagined Hagerty's unspoken thought. *Stay out of trouble.* He had every intention of keeping Catherine away from anything that might resemble trouble, but her sister was another matter.

The other message was from Kara to all of them when she'd arrived for her turn at the hospital. Doctor said things stable. Pain management is a big issue. No more than one visitor at a time. Staff unresponsive to bending any more rules, Chase, so stay away until your next shift, please.

No doubt the family was being cautioned on rules because Chase had already bent or broken many of them. It would probably have been better to send Kara for the first shift, but Chase did have medical training from his days in the Army, even if he lacked compliance.

Garrett noted that the worst of the storm had passed. Unfortunately, that would leave the uneven terrain slippery. Nothing could be done about that.

Kara's call caught him mid-yawn. He sat in the trailer's tiny kitchen and picked up.

"I didn't want to text this info. Sorry, Gare, but the socials provided by Orson were stolen. Most likely he bought synthetic IDs. The numbers trace back to two deceased children."

His heart sank. Fraudsters often used stolen SSNs to create identities with fake names and dates of birth. There was minimal risk that the crime would be discovered until years later if at all. He'd need to tell Catherine, but it would hit her hard. This morning was probably not the right moment. He thanked his sister, who promised to put it all in an email for his two siblings and Hagerty before she disconnected.

Catherine's uncle Orson had provided stolen identities, buying names for Catherine and Antonia to hide behind. Fake identities. He understood the power of a disguise. As Catherine had pointed out the previous evening, Garrett had his own mask, one he'd made himself.

The funny Garrett, the suave guy who always lightened the mood. Always the "good guy," the big brother whom people came to, the one who would provide a laugh. The charmer, the clown.

He stared out the moisture-covered window, the droplets morphing his reflection into the young man he used to be, the one who struggled to read, write, who was the best at sports, the quickest with a joke, always covering, always pretending.

If God loves you, then why do you have to cover up who you are?

He felt something expand and swell inside his chest. God knitted Garrett together, faults, foibles and all. He'd known it, but somehow Catherine's calling him out had made it so much more real.

You are precious to God. He made you. He loves you.

Even though he didn't learn like other people.

Even if he'd been wrong about Porter Stone.

Even if he'd let a killer go free.

That dug at his insides like a knife. Even if…he'd ruined things for a woman and her sister all those years ago.

You are precious to God. He made you. He loves you.

The real Garrett Wolfe, not the charming clown.

If Catherine could forgive him, he could forgive himself and quit hiding behind the Mr. Charming identity. There was such relief in it.

Lord, thanks for loving and forgiving. Please help me give Catherine her family back. When he heard the shower running, he fixed a pot of coffee and fueled up, plowing his way through a piece of toast and jam and setting another slice to toast for her. Catherine emerged, her hair pulled back in a neat twist. She was layered in jeans, a sweatshirt and a jacket borrowed from Stephanie. Smudges under her eyes made her skin appear even paler.

His pulse ticked up at the sight of her, one bare foot, propped up on the other, holding her boots and socks. How did she look graceful, sliding onto the bench seat and doing something as mundane as tugging on socks? And the way she tied the laces so precisely, double knotting so the loops were perfectly symmetrical? He lost track of the cooking until a blackened slice of bread popped out of the machine. "Uh, care for some toast?" He grinned. "Do-over. I can make you one that isn't incinerated, I'm pretty sure."

She shook her head. "No, thank you. My stomach is too uncooperative."

"Sure. I understand. No sweat. We have food in the go bags for later."

While she finished tying her boots, he gave her a rapid-fire weather report.

"Occasional showers beat the constant barrage we had yesterday," she said.

"Yep." He lured Pinky from the couch to the porch and strapped a waterproof search and rescue vest on him. The dog gave him an excited we've-got-a-job bonk with his nose.

An important job, Pink. Life or death.

He checked again to be sure the pillowcase he'd taken from the hospital with Antonia's scent on it was bagged and in his pack before they stepped out into the chilly predawn. He locked the trailer behind them.

Stephanie was already waiting at her car, arms crossed. Tank and Chloe eyeballed them through the rear window, the porch light gleaming off their noses.

By flashlight they double-checked the supplies and the weather report.

"Park ranger is expecting us." Stephanie illuminated her watch and checked the time again. His twin was annoyed and he didn't need to ask why.

Three minutes later, Chase emerged, yawning, a five-o'clock shadow on his chin and his curly hair askew. The porch light showed his boots laced together, hanging around his neck, and a slice of cold pizza in his hand. At least he'd gotten his waterproof socks on before he hurried out to them.

"You're late," Steph said.

"In some time zones, I'm massively early." He got into the passenger seat. "You drive. I'll sleep. Avoid the potholes."

Steph rolled her eyes and got in. Garrett loaded Pinky into the rear of his vehicle.

"Chase looks tired," Catherine said.

"He runs on his own time, but to be fair he was probably up pestering Kara about Mom's condition."

"How is she?"

He shared the morning report. "Kara will let us know if

there's a situation. I feel better knowing she's there. Chase has medical training, but he's, umm…"

"Light on diplomacy skills?"

He laughed, delighted with her description. "Definitely." There was not yet any hint of sunrise, but he was glad to see glimmers of clear dark sky between the moonlit clouds.

She worried her lower lip between her teeth as they left Whisper Valley behind.

He adjusted the heater. "Care to share your thoughts?"

"I was thinking about Tony, trying to imagine her plan. She's impulsive, but she usually has some sort of strategy. She'd probably set up a camp spot, maybe, prepare to hike to the cabin. Years ago she showed me a picture on her phone of her and Stone in front of the cabin. She said she told the cops about it when Stone first escaped but they found nothing. I wish I'd paid better attention. All I recall is 'no one around and tons of trees.' Which describes all of wilderness America, doesn't it?"

"Kara's continuing to try and glean what cabin that is, specifically, which friend of the Stones owns a property up there. She contacted the police but there was nothing in Stone's file to indicate exactly which cabins they'd searched a decade ago, unfortunately. She'll find something. I know it. She's a genius in her own way."

Catherine shoved her hands under her thighs. "Tony might have found a ride up there last night and decided to risk hiking in the dark to the cabin." She gulped. "What if she already found Stone and we're too late?"

"Highly unlikely she'd have gotten very far. The area around the Pacific Crest Trail is treacherous during the day, but at night, and during a storm, it'd be impossible to navigate without…" He was going to say "dangerous accidents" but he reconsidered. "If she's got some survival skills as you mentioned, she'd wait for daylight, move out early like we're doing."

"And when and if she does find him… I'm worried about what she'll do. Like Chase she's a little…light on diplomacy skills."

Though he wouldn't say it, he'd been mulling over the same thing. Tony was the proverbial loose cannon. Impulsive, angry behavior wasn't going to lend itself to a good outcome. "We'll do the best we can to keep everyone safe." It was a generic promise, easy to say, but he meant every syllable. He took in the strong set of her mouth, visualized the way her irises shifted between navy and cobalt. With a lurch, he realized that this woman, the woman who'd seen to the core of him and called him out of the shadows, was precious, a person he might very well love.

Love? His throat went dry and his palms damp as he hung on to the wheel. That was a thought to be examined later, much later, maybe never. Love, between two people with a past as twisted as theirs? His one and only semiserious love connection to date had ended when he let Stone escape. Whether from his shame or his girlfriend's, he wasn't sure.

Not the moment to knead that dough again as his father would say. For now, if it was in his power, Catherine would have her family returned to her safely that very day.

The road grew steeper as the hours passed. The tree-lined Highway 89 leading into the tiny town of Burney was not yet busy with visitors. At his brother's insistence, they bought coffee at a tiny drive-through shop built like a chalet. Chase and his massive, nitro-fueled coffee beverages. He grinned thinking about the scolding Stephanie would have provided their brother about the momentary delay.

Mist dampened his windshield. The cold weather would work in their favor to keep some of the tourists away, but not all. Burney Falls was a magnet from spring to fall and many preferred to experience the park when the crowds were thinner.

The park ranger met them at a bench outside the office. "I've gone over the logs. No camping check-in for a single woman last night, only groups and couples. She might have snuck in unnoticed and joined up with the tent campers."

Or she could have found a hollow of rock to keep dry for the night. How tough was she? Tough, he decided, like Catherine. There it was again, that surge of emotion. He gritted his teeth and refocused on the park ranger.

"As far as where Stone is keeping Orson, your search grids seem logical to me. Along the Pacific Crest Trail there are dozens of privately owned cabins folks rent out that are unoccupied. He could be hunkering down in one of them." He pointed to the map. "You can pick up the trail here, where it cuts through the park for about eighty miles. There's pretty dense foliage off the trail there in Shasta-Trinity Forest, but it's mostly below six thousand feet and the snow's pretty much gone, so that's a plus."

An enormous forest, an abducted man to find, as well as one reckless woman, and another to keep safe from a killer. They'd need all the advantages they could get. Stephanie thanked the ranger. Outside at a picnic table, they provided water and a snack for the dogs.

Stephanie gave them her I-mean-business look. "I don't need to do a safety briefing, do I? We all know what we're dealing with here. No one goes rogue. If there's any sign of a hot trail, we summon the other team. Check in every half hour."

"We got it. Basically don't be dumb," Chase said, cramming a Security Hounds baseball cap over his curls. "Message received."

They clipped long leads on their dogs and Garrett provided

Steph and Chase with Antonia's headband, which they'd acquired at Orson's property. Pinkerton would be following the hospital pillowcase with Antonia's scent. Too bad they didn't have an article from Stone, but he'd take what he could get.

What would the team find? Orson? Antonia? Stone? And what condition would they be in when they were located? He shot a glance at Catherine, chin high, brave and strong and scarred, silhouetted against the gray velvet of the sky.

She glanced in his direction and there was trust in that gaze.

Trust. And hope.

After everything, she trusted him. Without considering what his siblings might think, he held out a hand for one of hers and they started the search.

Catherine gradually warmed up as the rising sun chased the clouds away. The stretches of trail alternated between flat areas hemmed in by trees, to steep twisted miles revealing gorgeous spring-fed lakes. The beauty was inescapable, but it did not seep into her soul past the churning anxiety. Were they getting closer to her sister and uncle? Or moving in completely the opposite direction?

Pinkerton sniffed the pillowcase that Garrett offered. He flapped his ears, nostrils quivering, and set off down the trail.

Her heart soared. Her sister… Pinky must have picked up her trail.

He ambled, his attention caught by an aroma as they chugged along, then seemingly lost interest in an on-again off-again pattern. Catherine's frustration mounted but Garrett simply let Pinky rest, provided another fresh sniff of pillowcase, and a treat or two, and the dog regrouped. She estimated they'd hiked three miles. "Can a bloodhound really follow a scent this far?"

Garrett nodded. "For more than a hundred miles in some cases, even if the trail's old. They're relentless, which is a quality that probably landed Pinky here on death row before we found him."

"Death row? What do you mean?"

"Bloodhounds can be massively destructive, especially when they're young. Comes from their natural curiosity. Pinky was left in a shelter when he was eight months old. Adopted again and returned, after being chained in a backyard, which is where I believe he developed his fear of thunder. He'd lived in the shelter for close to a year when we snagged him right before he was scheduled to be euthanized. He was pretty shut down but look at him now." Pinky glanced over as if he knew he was being discussed. "He needed training, patience and a big space, but mostly he wanted a job, didn't you, boy?"

The thought of Pinky being chained and discarded made a lump form in her throat. "Did you train him yourself?"

"With help and guidance from Mom. And yes, I lost several pairs of shoes and a beautiful leather catcher's mitt before we forged an understanding."

Catherine giggled. "Surely you didn't do something like that, Pinky?"

"Don't let his boyish good looks fool you. He's a bulldozer in a fur coat." Pinky swerved along the trail, nose to the ground. "We used to breed bloodhounds, but when we realized there were so many good ones waiting for a chance, we switched to rescue mode."

Rescue mode. Fitting for the Security Hounds business. When a massive fallen tree covered the trail, they allowed Pinky to lead them around the blockade. Had her sister really gone this way?

Garrett slapped at a gnat buzzing around his face, straightening at a text. "It's Kara." She tensed at the excitement in his tone. He bent close to show her the message.

A former coworker of Bill Stone's owns a cabin. I'm including long/lat coordinates. I contacted Hagerty with this info as well.

Garrett pumped a fist. "Yes. Kara comes through. A break, finally."

Catherine blew out a breath. "At least we have something specific to go on now."

He put the coordinates into his phone. "And we're already moving in that direction, so it's a positive indication that Antonia was headed this way too. Awesome that we've got enough bars here." He called Chase's phone.

"Copy," Chase replied. "Our dogs have no hits so far in this grid anyway so we'll loop around toward your location. Hold in place at the coordinates until we get there. ETA forty."

Forty minutes seemed like an eternity, but the information fueled a faster pace. The trail grew steeper, less defined.

"If somebody does have a cabin here, they must like their solitude," she said, panting.

Garrett wiped his sweaty brow. "There's probably an easier trail somewhere for a vehicle, but that's not how Antonia approached, if Pinky's right."

Likely her sister would have gone with stealth.

Her calf muscles were screaming as Garrett called for a break. He gave Pinky a drink before downing half a water bottle and urging her to do the same. She didn't want to stop, not for one moment, but she knew he was right.

The sound of running water enveloped them as they continued, the ground rising in rocky peaks all around. They climbed to a clearing, where Pinky's tail thudded in overtime. Through a gap in the trees they spotted a small cabin and the sliver of a vehicle parked in the rear.

Her uncle's SUV. Her breathing ramped up even faster.

She started forward, but he caught her arm. "We have to wait. Steph and Chase will be here soon and Hagerty too, likely."

Agonized, she stared down at the structure. So still. She could not detect any human voices. Not surprising. A thunderous river roared in the background, funneling through a steep canyon to the side of the cabin.

Was Tony inside? In trouble? Uncle Orson? She felt Garrett's touch, fingers gripping her wrist. He didn't speak, but there was comfort in his presence.

"How much…?" Her words died on her lips as a gunshot pierced the air.

Garrett yanked her down, drawing his weapon and thrusting his phone at her. "Text my sister."

Fingers clumsy with fear, she pressed out a message just as the front door of the cabin slammed open. Stone appeared, running, head down. When he caught sight of Garrett he charged, yelling something over the tumult.

Garrett aimed. "Stop, Stone."

Stone blundered on, the whites of his eyes gleaming. Garrett was about to take a shot when Antonia appeared next, hair flying wild, a gun in her hand. Garrett could not risk missing and hitting Tony.

"No, Tony, don't," Catherine screamed, erupting from her hiding spot. If her sister shot now, she could hit Garrett or Pinky.

Oblivious, Tony sprinted after Stone, her next shot plowing into the dirt near Catherine's foot.

"Antonia, stop," Garrett yelled.

Stone didn't slacken. Pinky barked but Stone plowed right into Garrett as he ran toward the trail, sending Garrett stumbling backward toward the lip of the gorge.

She saw him teeter, arms flung wide, his mouth open in surprise, and then he fell out of sight.

With a panicked yelp, Pinkerton launched himself after his owner and disappeared.

TWELVE

Time stopped as Catherine stood frozen in shock. She wanted to scream at Stone and Antonia, but they continued their mad sprint, disappearing into the trees, and all she could think about was Garrett and Pinky. She lurched forward, falling, rocks biting into her knees before she regained her balance. When she skidded to the edge of the gorge, the ground crumbled under her boots. She flopped to her stomach. Her hair had come loose from the twist and she shoved it back, desperate to spot them.

Moisture thrown up from the river blinded her and she dashed a sleeve over her eyes. "Garrett!" There was no answer but the pounding water.

Stephanie and Chase arrived. She screamed out an update.

Chase immediately ordered Tank and Chloe to sit far enough away from the edge and crawled on hands and knees, passing her and easing over the side amid a cascade of rubble.

"Chase…" Stephanie yelled, to no effect. Catherine tried to keep him in view but the spray was impenetrable.

After an eternity, Chase popped back up. "I see him and Pinky. At my one o'clock. Ropes."

Catherine grabbed the end of the coil Stephanie tossed her. "Wrap it around that tree," Stephanie commanded.

She did so, heart thundering. The trees here were scrawny—

small specimens, willowy from the lack of sunlight. Would they hold? Stephanie encircled the only other nearby pine. Double protection. Catherine's lungs felt close to exploding. She shot a look to the far grove, praying she'd see her sister returning, unharmed, but no one appeared. *Just hold on to the rope. Get Garrett and Pinky to safety. Then worry about Antonia.*

Chase wrapped a harness around his waist and when Stephanie gave him the thumbs-up, he walked backward over the rocky lip, debris sliding down with him.

The rope tugged sharply under Chase's weight and she steadied herself, the tree at her back. A sharp crack split the air. The rope slithered in her palms.

She whipped around. The tree trunk where Stephanie was anchored had buckled. Stephanie struggled, but the rope slid loose, spraying bits of wood.

Stephanie grimaced. "I'm losing it—hold on, Catherine."

Catherine threw herself forward and strained against the rope, looping a section around her waist. The tree trunk trembled under the load, bending until it broke with an audible snap.

Stephanie yelled something and lunged for the rope but there wasn't enough time.

When the slack played out, Catherine was hauled toward the gorge along with the splintered branches. She sought something, anything, to stop her progress. Chase, Garrett and Pinky would have no chance and she would join them as they plummeted onto the sharp rocks. With all her strength she dug her heels into the ground. She skidded helplessly, her boots plowing through the loose detritus until she slammed up against a strong shelf of granite.

The strain intense, she planted her body. The rope dug into her sides as it worked to pull her over the edge. Was Stephanie close? She couldn't tell. There was only the pain and her desperate need to save Garrett, Pinky and Chase. When she thought she could withstand the weight no longer, the pressure suddenly eased. Stephanie was at her shoulder with Hagerty. Their combined effort was enough for Stephanie to catch a spire of granite with the rope. Catherine and Hagerty kept the tension until Stephanie could tie it off.

The three of them ran to the edge of the gorge.

Water billowed up from below and blurred her vision. Garrett? Pinky? She searched for Garrett's jacket amid the torrent or a glimpse of Pinky's harness. Chase? With each passing second her nerves knotted tighter. Where were they?

"There." Stephanie pointed to a position to her right. "Chase is waving like he's a rock star, the dork," she said, half-bending in relief. "Haul you out when you give us a signal," she shouted.

Chase offered a thumbs-up and turned his back to them. Catherine finally spotted Garrett's dark hair, soaked and dripping, over Chase's shoulder. He was tucked onto a ledge with Pinky clutched to his side like an overgrown toddler. The dog appeared to be alert. The relief made her sag. Garrett was alive. Pinky was too. *Thank You, God.*

But what else had transpired while she'd been frantic to secure Garrett? The ring of the gunshots and Antonia's stark expression as she'd run by clutching the gun flooded back. Tony was as reckless as she'd feared in her desire to capture Stone. Why had it seemed to her sister like a good idea to pursue a murderer instead of waiting for help?

Her stomach twisted. Because of what she'd discovered in the cabin? Catherine shut down the thought immediately. Her energy was focused on getting Garrett out before he became hypothermic. The water tossed up from the river at Chase and Garrett was frigid, no matter the season. And hypothermia attacked quickly.

When Chase finally gave them the thumbs-up, Stephanie, Catherine and Hagerty used a winch on the front of Hagerty's vehicle and a sturdy nylon rope to hoist them clear. Chase unclipped immediately, seemingly no worse for wear as he untied Garrett.

"Let go of the pooch, bro," he told Garrett. "Pinky's fine."

It looked like a physical effort for Garrett to release his dog. Pinky shook his coat, spraying them all with moisture. Stephanie called Pinky but he would not come. Instead, the dog licked the water from Garrett's face.

Garrett sat up, blinking. "That was worse than the flashbang grenade." He sought Catherine out first. "Anyone hurt?"

She allowed herself to breathe finally. "I—I don't think so. Tony ran after Stone and…" She couldn't help her gaze from going to the cabin. Uncle Orson was the unknown.

"I've got a helicopter launching to track Stone and Antonia," Hagerty said. "I'll go…"

But the words didn't impact Catherine as she stood. Garrett was okay. Chase and Pinky were too. But what was waiting for her in that cabin? She flashed on the doctor who'd delivered the report that her father had indeed died on that dreadful day ten years before. His expression, the pity, the horrible facts that once said could never be forgotten. Her future and her sister's hung on every syllable.

She would not, could not, wait again for news to be delivered to her while she sat passively, torturously wondering. Not this time.

She rose, turned, walked…and then she was sprinting, ignoring the calls from the people behind her. Slipping once on the damp flagstones took her to a knee, but she was up again in an instant. Through the open door, into a musty living room covered in wood paneling and a kitchen with crumpled fast-food bags and empty soda cans.

She wanted to shout for her uncle, but her terror would not allow the words to pass her throat. *Please, please, please...* One empty bedroom, a bare mattress, past a tiny bathroom with a rust-stained toilet bowl, toward one closed door at the end of the hallway.

Please...

Hand shaking, she turned the knob.

The inside was dark, the window shade closed. It took her eyes a moment to clear.

Orson was lying on the bed, blindfolded, his wrists and ankles fastened to the bed posts with dirty loops of rope. There were several candy bar wrappers on the floor and a half-empty gallon-size bottle of water. His clothes were rumpled, and smelled of sweat, and his mouth was slack. He jerked toward the sound of her approach.

Gratitude flooded her soul. He was alive. Tears welled and her limbs quivered. "Uncle Orson." She collapsed next to the bed.

"Cathy?" His voice was a croak.

"Yes. It's me." Tears trickled unchecked down her cheeks as she patted his chest. "You're okay. We'll get you to a hospital." She was fumbling to undo the knot around his wrist when Hagerty, Stephanie and Chase entered, and with them Garrett, who was holding Pinky and clutching a silver emergency blanket around them both. Stephanie gently pushed Catherine aside.

"Let me." She pulled a folding knife from her pocket and sawed at the restraints while Catherine eased off the blindfold.

Uncle Orson blinked and knuckled his eyes with his free hand. "Didn't think I was going to see you again, Cathy."

"I never doubted for a moment," she said, unable to stop her tears.

* * *

Garrett's knees knocked with relief and the trauma of his recent fall. He was banged and bruised, freezing in spite of the blanket, but finding Orson alive overrode his discomfort.

Catherine hugged her uncle fiercely, helping him to sit up. Hagerty handed him a bottle of water, urging him to drink. He was clumsy, weak, and he dropped the bottle, splashing the mattress. "Where's Tony?"

Catherine was trying to control her emotions so Garrett answered for her. "She ran out. After Stone."

Orson groaned. "He kept me locked inside the SUV for I don't know how long with my hands and feet tied up and a blanket over me. It was so hot in there and I was tumbled like laundry in the dryer. He let me out every so often to give me water and food and let me relieve myself. Left me in the woods somewhere too, tied to a tree. I'm not sure what day he brought me here but the whole time he ranted about her. Said he'd do whatever it took, abduct you even, if it meant he could get to her. He's obsessed. I wondered if I was hallucinating when I heard her voice through the door. I hoped I was anyway. She's no match for Stone. It was pure folly of her to come after him in the first place."

Garrett leaned forward. "What did they say while they were arguing, Mr. Hart? Could you understand any of it?"

He shook his head. "I couldn't hear many of the words, only the tone of voice. They were angry, shouting at each other. I heard him say 'make you pay' and then there was a gunshot." Orson blanched. "He didn't…?"

Catherine hastened to reassure him. "No, Antonia had the gun. She was the shooter. They both ran into the woods."

"And she missed him? All her bragging about being a crack shot." He rolled a shoulder and Catherine actually smiled.

"Tony's always been high on confidence, Uncle Orson."

"Don't I know it."

Hagerty pulled out a map. "Stone's on foot now, so we're at an advantage. Three trails from here and one's pretty well-traveled. I'll send my officers and the park ranger to canvass," Hagerty said. "Chopper will be our eyes in the sky."

Garrett shivered in spite of himself. "I'm going too as soon as I get into dry clothes. I've got a change in my car."

"No." Hagerty spoke calmly. "Civilians will muddy up the works."

Garrett's chin went up. "I still have some of my cop instincts. I'm not going to get in your way."

Hagerty's eyes narrowed. Whatever rapport they'd had was gone. "Negative. Lesson learned. Bad enough this all went down without us. I won't risk my cops by including outsiders again."

He bit back a hard remark. Outsiders, him in particular. Hagerty was right. Garrett would never escape the stain on his reputation. He'd paid for what happened with Stone and he was still paying for it.

Chase shook water from his hair. "Suggestion. How about Steph and Chloe? They're dry and she's former law enforcement, retired only recently. Consulted on cases with your partner, right? So you know she's sharp on the skills."

Garrett kept the mortification from his expression. If Security Hounds could be involved in any way, render some aid in catching Stone or retrieving Antonia, then he'd take it without argument.

Hagerty frowned. "We—"

"Won't be able to track nearly as well as a bloodhound," Steph interjected. She picked up a man's sweat sock. "Stone's, I take it. Chase can track Antonia once he's clear here and I'll go after Stone. How are your cops at following scent cones?"

Hagerty scowled and snagged his radio. "Come with me and we'll find a staging area."

Garrett watched them go without comment as they waited for an ambulance. Catherine hovered by her uncle's side, talking quietly, smoothing his hair, urging him to sip water. Garrett kept an arm around Pinky.

"How's my sweet boy?" he murmured. "You okay?" The dog shoved his unwieldy torso closer to Garrett. "You didn't have to dive in after me. Next time run for help or something, okay?" He kissed Pinky's damp brow and snuggled him closer.

When the medics arrived, Catherine stepped away and moved to Garrett. Pinky lathered her wrist with his tongue.

She stroked his ears. "Are you both warmed up?"

He smiled. "Toasty."

"Feel okay?"

"Sure, why wouldn't I?" He caught her frown and took a breath that hurt his ribs. "Wait. That was the court jester thing. Actually, I'm..."

She waited while he searched for the words.

"Grateful that Pinky didn't get hurt diving in for me. Or Chase. Frustrated that we didn't get to Stone and your sister. Sad," he said finally, "not to be helping with the search." *And humiliated.* He left that one out.

"I can't believe it worked out like that either but I know Steph and Chloe will track them." She held out her hand. "And I'm so relieved that you two aren't hurt."

He allowed himself to rest his cold cheek against her palm, feeling the scratches where the rope had burned her. She'd done everything she could to help rescue them, him. It pumped a strange warm adrenaline through his veins. "I know Steph and Chloe will come through. I just... I can't help thinking if I'd done things differently..."

She stroked his cheek, leaning close enough that he could barely resist the urge to kiss her. While he hesitated, she startled him by inching forward and kissing him, her lips light as a breeze on his.

"I thank God that you and Pinky aren't hurt," she whispered. "For now I'm going to be grateful for that."

And all he could do was look into the dark sea of her eyes as his own heart bumped and pitched in his chest.

"We're ready to transport," a medic called.

She squeezed his shoulder and returned to her uncle.

Garrett intentionally did not make eye contact with Chase, whom he knew had witnessed the kiss and was no doubt ready to tease him mercilessly. At least Stephanie had gone outside to talk things over with Hagerty. Garrett wasn't sure why the friendly kiss had made everything go shaky inside, but he wasn't about to dissect it with his older brother.

Nonetheless, when Chase walked by Garrett caught an elbow to the side. "'Bout time you got yourself a nice girl," Chase teased. "Mom will be thrilled."

Garrett groaned, but Steph called to Chase, cutting off Garret's denial.

How could he ignore that she was in his every thought? That she was the only one on the planet who made him want to stop hiding behind Mr. Charming? Refute the notion that anything happening to her shot a quiver of terror right to his soul? What was he feeling about Catherine Hart exactly? He was still mulling that over as they loaded Orson into a rescue vehicle.

A medic looked Garrett over. "How about we transport you too?"

"No, thank you." As long as his dog was okay, he could warm up on his own. He checked Pinky again, and offered treats, delighted when the dog slurped them up. "You're Daddy's brave boy, aren't you?"

Chase looked over, his disgust clear. "He's a working dog. Quit talking to him like a toddler." His dog, Tank, observed in that standoffish way from his spot in the sun.

Garrett continued to fondle Pinky's ears. "This is why Pinky and I are bonded and you and Tank are surly acquaintances." Not exactly the truth. Tank was the kind of dog that didn't crave the love and affection Pinky did, but it was tit for tat with Chase.

"Whatever. We get the job done with our self-respect intact."

"You do you," Garrett said, but the tease fell flat. He was worried about Stone and Antonia. And his mother. Worry was not his go-to, so he wasn't quite sure why the feelings weighed on him like paving stones.

A cop delivered his go bag from the car and he changed in a back room of the cabin. He removed Pinky's wet harness and rubbed him down one more time to be sure he was completely dry before they rejoined the others. Catherine accepted his offer of a ride to the hospital.

Kara's text came just as he loaded Pinky into the car.

Mom's groggy but stable. She asked about the search.

Garrett let out a whoosh of air and texted back. I'll be there tonight to relieve you. But as he started the engine, he already knew he was going to work a deal with Chase to split the time with whatever sibling was available. Stone was still at large.

He'd be there for his mom and for the Hart sisters.

Somehow.

THIRTEEN

Catherine shifted and wiggled in the hard waiting-room chair, palms sore from rope burn. Garrett brought her a bottle of water and Pinky sprawled at her feet, a fleshy puddle on the cool linoleum. "Has Stephanie called?"

Garrett sighed and she braced for bad news. "Yes. It would appear Stone stole a motorcycle. Chloe lost him at that point. Chase and Tank caught your sister's trail, which continued on back to the campground. A witness heard her bumming a ride off someone who was leaving."

She groaned. "Why does my sister have to behave like some sort of commando? Doesn't she realize she's putting us all in a terrible position? She's been wild since my dad died. Uncle Orson tried his best to set limits, but he doesn't have father skills and I don't think either one of us would have accepted him trying anyway." Pinky nuzzled her knee and she patted him.

"I've heard that people can occasionally get psychologically stuck at the age when a terrible trauma occurred."

"I hate to think of that since Tony was a rebellious sixteen at the time. Dad always said she was a hurricane in a cute little bottle." She examined Garrett, noted the bruise forming at his temple. "Are you sure you're okay? If you need to go home…"

"I don't."

His expression was so genuine, almost as if he felt like he *was* home, with her. Imagination, she scolded. But still, her heart beat a tick faster. Simple gratitude? she wondered. But nothing felt simple about her feelings for Garrett Wolfe.

A nurse gave her permission to enter her uncle's room.

"I'll wait right here," Garrett said.

Uncle Orson looked frail in the big hospital bed, pale and depleted from his ordeal. She kissed him and he squeezed her hand. "Awww, Cathy. What a muddled mess, isn't it? Any word on Tony?"

She didn't want to alarm him any more by revealing that Antonia had hitched a ride to parts unknown. "She's still on the loose somewhere and so is Stone."

"She won't give up until she gets what she's after. This is all a complete nightmare." He shook his head. His eyes went damp and he blinked hard. "After your father was killed, I just wanted so badly to protect you girls, to keep you from any more wounds. I did things wrong."

She reached to console him but he waved off her touch.

"I shouldn't have bought those IDs but I was terrified after Stone escaped that he'd find you both. Tony'd told me how obsessive he was, and she was determined to move away and stay with the family she knew and finish her schooling on-line. Made sense, after what happened, but she didn't have us around to keep her in check."

Catherine remembered those tortured conversations with her sister...

"I'm going. You should too," Tony had said.

"I don't want to leave Uncle Orson," Catherine had replied.

"Stay if you want, but I don't have a choice. Porter will never leave me alone and anyway I can't stand the way everyone looks at us now," her sister had explained. "I want to go live where nobody knows what happened."

She'd felt it too, how the people whispered to each other when she passed. Their furtive glances were full of pity. In the aftermath of the murder her identity had changed to "that poor girl." She would forever be seen through that new lens.

Catherine sagged, suddenly exhausted, but forced a fortifying breath and raised her chin. Everything was spinning out of control again, but she would never let Orson feel guilty. "You did your best. No one could have asked for more."

His laugh was bitter. "Linda doesn't think so. She's divorcing me, you know."

"I, uh, I did know that." She had to tell him about her last encounter with Linda. "Uncle Orson, do you know that she's in a relationship with Tom Rudden, your security service guy?"

His lips thinned and a rosy flush crept into his cheeks. "No surprise, really. I had a suspicion. Saw them together a time or two, whispering and laughing as if I was too dense to notice. He doesn't have many scruples, but that's worked to my advantage upon occasion. Has she been busy swiping whatever she wants from the house while I was trying to stay alive?"

Catherine had to nod. "I'm really sorry to ask, but you don't…?" She swallowed. How could she verbalize it? But how could she not? With so much at stake? "Do you think Linda and Rudden had anything to do with your kidnapping?"

He quirked an eyebrow and she hurried on.

"Like maybe they conspired with Stone for him to abduct you? They made some sort of dirty deal to get you out of the way? Rudden might have disabled the security system himself."

He grinned, swiping at his sweaty forehead. "Nah. That's a clever theory, but Linda wouldn't bother with a plan that might possibly get her hands dirty. She's going to take me to the cleaners for every dime. She's already got the lawyers lined up. That's her strategy."

The suspicion still nagged at her. *But wouldn't it be easier for Linda if Orson was dead?* Pressing the point did not seem beneficial at the moment. He looked worse than when she'd found him in the cabin—his skin had an unhealthy gray tint and his forehead was glossed with perspiration. "Do you want some water, Uncle Orson? Are you too warm?"

He ignored her questions. "You're in town until Stone's arrested and Tony's back?"

She nodded. "And until you're completely better and out of here. Yes."

"Where are you staying?"

"At the Security Hounds Ranch, temporarily."

His eyes narrowed. "No. Go stay at the house. I'll send someone to take care of the security system and hire a bodyguard. You'll be safe there."

"Security Hounds is taking good care of me."

His brow furrowed. "You realize you're staying with the guy who let Stone escape?"

Catherine's cheeks went hot. "Garrett feels terrible about that."

He snorted. "Oh, sure he does. I can tell he's all over broken up about hurting our family. A real stand-up guy, that Garrett Wolfe."

His sudden anger confused her. "What's wrong, Uncle Orson?"

"Nothing."

"It's not nothing. What aren't you telling me?"

"Wolfe couldn't protect you back then. The cops were

useless, so I took matters upon myself and now he's trying to make me pay for that."

"Pay how?"

He rubbed at his chest. "This Security Hounds outfit tipped off the cops that I broke the law in acquiring those IDs. Two officers have already been here and asked me a couple of questions before the doctors shooed them out. They're coming back this afternoon. They want to know my source, but I won't divulge it because they might uncover other things I've paid this individual to do. Nothing terrible. Nothing like abduction or murder. Nice of the cops, huh? That's what I've got to look forward to as I recover from being kidnapped? Jail?"

Fury flashed through her. The cops were badgering her uncle? When there was a killer running loose? "That's terrible."

"It sure is. Treating me like I'm the criminal here." His face flushed, then turned ashen. He began to gasp for air.

She shot to her feet. "Uncle Orson?"

He grimaced in pain and alarms began to beep. Frantic, she pressed the button for help but there was already a nurse rushing in and urging her away from the bed and out of the room. Several more raced up with a cart, their expressions grave.

Catherine went dizzy. This could not be happening. Garrett and Pinky hustled up and eased her into a chair. Garrett held on to her arm.

"I think…he's having a heart attack," she said.

"The medical team's the best here. They'll help him. I'm so sorry."

Nerves prickling, she yanked her arm free. "Are you? Sorry?"

He frowned at her acid tone. "Yes, of course. I know how much you love your uncle and he's been through a lot."

"Yes, he has. The man was held captive until today and yet your Security Hounds couldn't wait to inform the police that he'd broken the law, could they?"

Garrett raised an eyebrow. "This is about the social security numbers? We looked into that, as I told you we would. Once we found that they were stolen, we had no choice but to turn over the info. We can't conceal knowledge of a crime from the police."

She wanted to scream, to slam her palm into the wall. "What does it matter, a couple of numbers?"

Garrett's calm demeanor infuriated her further.

"He paid someone for the social security numbers of deceased children. It's called ghosting. I know this comes at a bad time."

Her mouth trembled with anger. "A bad time? You think? What my uncle did was wrong. He shouldn't have paid for stolen numbers, but he did it to protect us after our father was *murdered* and Stone went free. He knew we'd never be safe and he was right."

Garrett flinched. "I absolutely understand, but it's still a crime and Hagerty's got to take a look at that and turn it over to the FTC. It would have been better to wait until your uncle was feeling better, but he has to examine everything, follow each lead to track Stone down and he can't wait for an opportune moment."

She felt like laughing at the absurdity of it. One man was a killer and Orson was merely a loving, grief-stricken uncle. "Uncle Orson's not the criminal here, Garrett. He was abducted, could have been killed, and now that he's been interrogated and possibly had a heart attack, I could lose him…" She was annoyed that her voice wobbled.

"Catherine, I'm sorry this is all happening. I…"

She stood, wishing she'd never returned to Whisper Valley, never laid eyes on Garrett Wolfe again. "Why don't you go visit your mother?" she snapped. "I'd like to be alone now while I wait for word on my uncle's condition."

He rose and Pinky whined uncertainly. "Is there someone I can get to sit with you?" he said quietly.

She could barely get the answer out. "Who would that be exactly, Garrett? My dad's dead and my sister is risking her life by tracking his killer. I have no one." Her voice broke on the last word.

"Catherine…"

The hurt storming her muscles left her reckless. "I'll come by the ranch and grab my things from the trailer when I can."

"I understand you're angry, but please don't make a rash decision."

"I'll make whatever decisions I need to for myself and my family, what's left of it. I'm going to stay at my uncle's house."

He started to shake his head. "That's not safe."

"I'll lock all the doors and call the police if I need help." Her words felt incendiary, like each one burned as it came out of her mouth and sizzled into Garrett. "I can at least protect his property while he's in here. Maybe my sister will show up there and I can help her too, unless you think *she* should also be arrested for trying to protect us."

He looked suddenly battered and exhausted. She felt a flicker of guilt but it did not dampen her fiery rage.

"If that's what you want," he said finally.

"Nothing that's happened since I was seventeen is what I wanted," she choked out. Furiously she blinked back tears. "Go back to your family, Garrett."

And she was left alone to pray that God would spare what was left of hers.

* * *

In a daze, Garrett found his way to his mother's beside on the next floor up. Though she appeared tired and tentative, her examination was as sharp as ever.

"Are you going to tell me what's happened?" she said.

"Everything's fine."

"No, it's not."

He kissed her. "Glad you're feeling better, Grand Inquisitor."

"Better enough that I can tell you're upset. I heard what happened at the cabin already, but what else don't I know?"

He sighed and repeated some of the conversation he'd had with Catherine, her decision to leave Security Hounds. "She blames me."

"She's hurt. Scared."

"That's what kills me. It's just like she felt ten years ago, Mom. Hurt. Scared, and I couldn't help. In fact I made it worse."

She reached for his hand and Pinky intercepted by shoving his wet nose in first so she scrubbed him between the ears. "I don't understand what the cop job is like, Garrett. I never wanted to be a cop. But what I am certain of is that you are a man who follows God, tries his best, always does the right thing, even if it's painful. That hasn't changed."

His gaze dropped to the floor. "I'm not sure I did the right thing all those years ago with Stone."

"Yes, you are. Your gut is still telling you there's something off, even if your heart is screaming that it's not worth the pain to listen."

"Preach it, Mom." Garrett turned to find Chase leaning against the doorway.

"I know it's only one visitor at a time, but I'm going to

kick little brother out so we'll be in compliance," Chase said. "'Cuz they're all uppity about the rules in this place."

"But I just got here," Garrett protested.

Chase pointed to the door. "Bring it outside. We're not supposed to argue in front of our mother."

She laughed. "Like that ever stopped you before."

In the hallway, Chase spoke first. "I heard you say Catherine's leaving. I wasn't eavesdropping, you were just blabbing too loud to notice when I cleared my throat to signal you I was there."

"Things fell apart." Completely. Utterly.

"I got that impression. So you have work to do. I'll stay here with Mom."

Garrett opened his mouth to protest but Chase shrugged him off. "Your instincts are telling you the same thing mine are. We're not done with this and Catherine isn't safe until Stone is captured again. Now that she's not under our immediate purview and too angry to accept our help, she's even more at risk."

It felt good to know that his brother shared his concern, that he wasn't being buffeted around by paranoia or past guilt. There was something strange happening that he could not pin down, an uneasy electricity cascading through his gut. "Thanks. I'll go arrange security at her uncle's. Someone other than Tom Rudden's company."

"Nope. You do it."

"Do what?"

"Stay there, at Orson's."

He blinked. "She won't want me there."

"So don't tell her. Watch from afar. Do your sneaky undercover thing and keep an eye on the place."

"You think something's going down."

"I don't know, but you'll never forgive yourself if you

aren't there for her and I don't want to hear you whining for the rest of your life."

He'd ended with the jab, but Garrett saw through the glib tone to the pain that his brother carried around since he'd lost the woman he loved.

"Chase…"

"No offense, but I'm pining for some coffee. Good talk. I'll brief Stephanie and Kara. Catch you later." He walked away, posture straight and chin up so only someone who'd known Chase for a long time would detect the slight hunch, as if there was a tender place he was trying to protect. Trying and failing.

Catherine's words cut him deeply.

My dad's dead and my sister is risking her life by tracking his killer. I have no one. He'd had fleeting daydreams that he'd become her ally, friend and maybe more. Was there anything left of the fragile stitches that had connected them? Unlikely, but he'd find out for sure, and keep her safe in the meanwhile.

Pinky flapped his ears and Garrett bent to caress him. "We're going to help get her life back, Pink."

And the first step was making sure no harm came to her at Orson's house.

FOURTEEN

Catherine roamed the hospital halls in a fog. She couldn't push Garrett out of her mind, or the uncertainty about her uncle's status. How could she get Orson back only to lose him? And how had she allowed herself to fall for a man who could send her uncle to jail if he survived? Her uncle had only been trying to protect his nieces. Wasn't there some leniency due?

Though she didn't remember buying it, somehow she had a cup of bitter coffee in her aching fingers. The sharp taste revived her somewhat and the walk at least soothed her muscles. She headed back to her uncle's room to check on him again. Her stomach dropped when she saw Tom Rudden leaning over the bed.

She rushed in. "What are you doing?"

He jerked around. "The hospital called Linda about the heart attack. I told her I'd check on him."

"Why? You don't have any affection for my uncle and neither does Linda."

He shrugged. "I've worked for Orson for more than a decade. Just checking in, like I said." He edged around her.

Checking in? No way did she believe that. She thought about her uncle's comment that Rudden had no scruples, yet he'd worked for Orson for a decade. A thought occurred to her. "Did you do any work for my uncle besides security?"

Rudden paused. "I took care of business for him and the people he loved. That's all."

What was he trying not to say? Before she had a chance to ask, he hurried off.

She brushed a finger across her uncle's cheek. *Business for him and the people he loved.* Orson had always been their life preserver. Without him, she and Antonia would have crumbled after their father's murder. But there were things about her uncle she didn't know, that much was certain. And Rudden was hiding something.

She leaned over, examining his lined face before she kissed him on the cheek. "I love you, Uncle Orson. No matter what."

Hours later, assured that the hospital would alert her at the slightest change, Catherine lugged her backpack into the grand front foyer of her uncle's house. She'd gained access using the key he'd given her years before. The rain had returned, making the afternoon gloomier, or maybe it was the mess in her heart coloring the world around her.

Uncle Orson was stable and that's about the best that could be said of the prognosis. The heart attack had caused some damage, which they were striving to reverse, but he was still not conscious. At least he'd given her permission to stay in the house before he'd been stricken. She might as well live publicly as Catherine Hart. There was no longer any protection from Stone or the wagging town tongues in an illegally provided alias.

So here you are, Catherine. Left to manage things on your own.

Her decision, though, wasn't it? Her stomach flipped when she considered how she'd cut down Garrett at the hospital. It hadn't been fair, of course, but a wound had ripped open when she felt her uncle threatened and she'd lashed out. She'd apologize, but their relationship would not return to what it had been. The wounds would take time to heal, if they ever did, and it felt awfully like she was back at square one. Fear and grief, loneliness and pain.

She made sure to lock the door behind her before dumping her pack on the sofa. The living room was spotless and stuffy, showing no clue of the previous violence. Just a few days ago Stone had pushed his way onto the property and abducted her uncle. The thought made her go cold all over. Tea. A nice steamy cup of tea would chase her chill away. Pattering to the kitchen, she stopped suddenly before pushing through the swinging door.

Talking?

Someone was in the kitchen of her uncle's house. Could Antonia have returned? There hadn't been any cars parked in the drive.

Heart thumping, she picked up a vase from the coffee table in case it wasn't her sister and eased the door open.

Linda was stirring a cup of coffee with one hand, her cell on speakerphone on the table.

"We have plenty of time," she said.

It was Rudden who answered. "You never know with heart attacks."

Linda looked up and they locked gazes.

Linda squeaked, shoving her hand to her chest. "You scared me."

"What are you doing here?" Catherine said. "I didn't see your car."

Linda spoke into her phone. "I'll call you back." She disconnected. "In answer to your question, this is my house, legally, not yours, and Tom dropped me off."

"I thought you'd moved out. And Uncle Orson said I could stay here."

"Before or after he had the heart attack?" She glared. "Like I said, I'm legally his spouse, so I'm kept informed."

Catherine closed her eyes, struggling for control. When she opened them, she was startled to see Linda watching her with a touch of compassion.

"Look, Catherine," she said with a sigh, "let's start over. I always respected you for telling Orson you didn't need a monthly stipend. It showed character and backbone. I admire a backbone in anyone. We don't have to be enemies. There's plenty of room in the house and I'm not staying over anyway. I only came to pack up some of my books from the study. I'll be another couple of hours, tops, so we can coexist for that long."

She'd hoped she'd be fortunate enough not to cross paths with Linda while the woman was scavenging her uncle's belongings. Was Linda being agreeable to trick her? Had she been plotting with Rudden before she'd been interrupted? Perspiration beaded on Catherine's brow as she remembered Rudden hovering over her uncle's bed. Was it even safe for her to stay?

Linda was already done with the conversation. She picked up a cardboard box and walked away to the study. Catherine scurried to the downstairs guest room and locked herself in. She had her cell phone, and she was safe behind a sturdy oak door. There was no immediate threat. She thought about texting Garrett to tell him about Linda's presence. The idea touched off a cascade of prickly emotions.

She'd made it clear she didn't want him around. It wasn't fair to send him mixed messages as if he was a bodyguard at her beck and call. She'd dug a hole and now she'd lie in it, at least until morning.

Fortunately, the guest room was well appointed with its own en suite bathroom, so she treated herself to a hot shower. Stomach growling, she ate the granola bars from the supply Garrett had insisted she pack for their wilderness search. For the millionth time, she wondered about her sister. Where was she? Would she ever give up her self-appointed quest? The hours ticked slowly by and she did not hear any sounds that Linda had left.

The hospital had no updates when she called. Antonia didn't respond to any of her messages either. Sleep, she figured, would be elusive, but she lay down anyway on the soft mattress. The events of the day pressed upon her until she felt her eyelids grow heavy...

With a lurch, she blinked awake. The bedside clock read 7:15 p.m. She fought off the stupor. *Way to stay alert, Cath.* A rustling sound yanked her to a sitting position. What had she heard? She hurried to the window and eased the curtain aside. The view revealed a darkened slice of the side yard, heavy with bushes, pools of landscape lighting painting the foliage silver.

A shadow glided along and she froze until it came closer and she realized it was an animal, a dog. Not just any dog. Pinkerton's ungainly form trotted from bush to bush, nose fixed to the ground, leash trailing behind him in the grass. How had he gotten there? And where was Garrett? He would never have left Pinky wandering. Worry wormed deep into her gut. Had he been hurt somehow?

Breath constricted, she jammed her feet into shoes, unlocked the bedroom door and hurried down the hallway to the exit that took her out into the side yard. The evening was hushed, her own feet sounding loud as she jogged over the grass.

"Pinky?" she said, half whisper, half yell.

She heard Pinky whine. When she caught up, he was standing still, staring toward the low stone retaining wall that separated the side yard from the broad sweep of gardens at the rear of the house.

"Pinky," she said again. He didn't even glance at her, completely fixated on whatever he was tracking. Could Garrett be prowling the property? She reached the dog, kneeled and put an arm around his quivering sides. He stiffened and the hair on his scruff went up. She heard it too. Footsteps from beyond the retaining wall. Coming closer.

Garrett? But Pinky would not be reacting so strangely if it was his partner.

She suddenly realized how foolish she'd been, leaving the protection of the house. She could have texted Garrett, called him to solve the mystery. Instead she was outside, alone.

She tried to coax Pinky away, but he was immobile.

The footsteps stopped. Her heart hammered when they started up again, moving in her direction. She grabbed Pinky's leash and hauled with all her strength to drag the heavy dog away from the intruder. Finally, Pinky seemed to come to his senses and sped after her until they were steps away from the door. She'd get him inside. Figure it out. Find Garrett. If she couldn't, she'd call Steph or Chase. She reached for the door when someone touched her arm.

With a yelp, she whirled to find Garrett, wide-eyed.

"What are you doing here?" she whispered.

"Tell you later. What's wrong?"

"I found Pinky wandering and I went to get him. There's someone in the yard behind the stone wall."

Garrett collected Pinky's leash and opened the door to the house. "I'll check it out. You wait inside." He escorted her in.

"Linda's here, or at least she was. I'm not sure now."

"Okay, I'll—"

A woman's scream pierced the air. Pinky yanked free from Catherine's hand and bolted into the hallway. Instinctively she ran after him.

"No," Garrett yelled.

Her common sense returned as they neared the front door. She slowed. Garrett snagged her wrist. Pinky sped ahead and disappeared in the direction of her uncle's study.

"Go outside to my car," Garrett insisted. "Call nine-one-one."

She was reaching for the front door when it crashed open. Tom Rudden stood on the threshold. "I heard a scream. What was that? Linda called me to pick her up."

A gunshot exploded from the end of the hallway. She cried out, felt Garrett's hands propelling her from the house. Before she'd cleared the threshold, Linda appeared in the study doorway and stepped into the hall. Her mouth was open, hand pressed to her red shirt. Pinky whined and circled her, trying to paw her thigh.

"Linda?" Rudden called. "Are you okay?"

Catherine thought Linda was going to say something, until her head tipped back and she collapsed. With a flash of nausea, Catherine realized it wasn't a red shirt Linda was wearing, but a white one, saturated with blood from the bullet wound in her chest.

Garrett made sure Catherine was locked in his car with Pinky and calling 911 before he returned to the house. Rudden refused to leave Linda's side and there wasn't much he could do about that since he wasn't law enforcement.

He made double sure the shooter was gone before he attempted first aid. Linda was clearly already dead, Rudden mumbling over her incoherently, but Garrett snagged a blanket and ordered Rudden to apply it to her wound anyway, in case he was wrong. If nothing else, it would keep Rudden occupied.

He returned to the study to examine the scene, staying in the doorway to take photos. The French doors were open, windblown rain spattering the hardwood floor. The shooter had gone in and out that way, likely. Wouldn't have been hard to force the lock, if it had actually been secured. The killer had probably chosen the French doors in the garden because they'd be concealed from sight. A carved wooden box, the size of a bread loaf, had tumbled open on the floor. He surmised it had been kept in the small cubbyhole, partially obscured by the ottoman, which had been knocked over. He dialed Stephanie.

"Is the scene secure?" she demanded.

"Shooter's gone," he answered, then reported on Rudden and Catherine.

Steph blew out a breath. "Why Linda?"

"Dunno. Could be a robbery. There's a box dumped on the floor that is the right size for a stash of bills."

"This doesn't feel like a random robbery."

"To me either. We surmised it was Rudden and Linda in on a plan to steal from Orson, but now…"

"Maybe it was Linda and Stone working together and he double-crossed her," Steph said. "Or he came for his payment and she didn't deliver to his satisfaction."

"As good a theory as any."

"Okay, brother of mine. You're not convinced. I can hear it. Why?"

"There's something here that I'm missing. Nothing concrete…just this bell clanging in my brain."

"Keep working it. I'll update everyone and see what I can glean from the police radio."

He disconnected and stood quietly with Rudden, silently

praying for Linda. There had been too much blood already. After checking on Catherine, he answered all the questions from the cops when they arrived, but he kept his ears open as he did so.

"Meet me at the station," Hagerty said brusquely.

"Yes, sir," he said. "I'll drive Catherine."

She was silent during the ride, which left him steeped in his own thoughts. What was he missing? Maybe nothing at all. Perhaps it was what it seemed—a random robbery or Stone, who had surprised Linda. He'd need money and if he wasn't involving his family, he'd have to take desperate measures. Garrett wondered if Stone had caught up with Antonia and taken her gun. He felt a prickle of panic. If Stone had Antonia... Too many questions without answers.

He and Catherine settled in the police department waiting room. Catherine wrapped her arms around Pinky's neck. He longed to comfort her, but he wasn't sure his efforts would be welcomed. Not with the way they'd parted at the hospital.

Kara joined them, patting Catherine gently on the shoulder. "We weren't sure if you two needed any support. I thought I'd pop in and see."

He smiled at his sister and Pinky wagged his tail in her direction. "You brought food, didn't you?"

"Just some sandwiches for you two and a big dog biscuit for Pinks." She handed them each a sandwich. "I'm going to take him outside for a walk. See you in a bit."

He unwrapped his sandwich. "Vegan cheese, basil and tomato on sourdough," he said. "Chase would say it's missing the meat."

Though he wasn't hungry, he took a bite so Kara would feel appreciated.

Catherine picked at the crust.

When the silence became burdensome, he sighed. "I don't even know what to say."

She shoved her hair behind her ear and blew out a slow breath.

He tensed.

"You can say you were right," she said. "It wasn't safe for me to stay at my uncle's house."

"Nobody likes an I-told-you-so, me first and foremost. You...had reasons for your decision."

She shook her head. "I can't understand. Why do you think Linda was killed?"

"Don't know, but the cops found some cash dropped outside the French doors, so it looks like a possible robbery."

"A random theft? Isn't that too much of a coincidence at this point?"

Exactly what he and his sister thought. He was hoping she wouldn't ask any more questions, but he could tell by the crimp in her eyebrows that she was spinning all the facts around.

"Was she shot with the same gun stolen from my uncle's house?"

"Not answerable until the ballistics come back."

He knew what she was thinking. Porter Stone had killed again. After he'd captured Antonia?

"Why were you outside, with Pinky running loose?"

He considered how to frame the explanation and prayed he wouldn't make things worse. "I felt uncomfortable knowing you were out there without security. Pinky and I decided to pull a night shift. He saw a raccoon and got away from me. He can't stand raccoons. I think he figures they wear masks so they must be shifty." The joke fell flat. He cleared his throat. "You made it clear you wanted to be alone, so I hope that I haven't offended you by inviting myself onto Orson's property."

She shook her head and gave him a defeated smile. "That'd be pretty silly of me to be offended instead of grateful that you were there. I'm grateful and…apologetic. I shouldn't have reacted that way at the hospital."

"No apology necessary."

"Yes, I think there is. I can't even believe what's happened to my life in the last four days. I hardly know what's going to come out of my mouth next."

She shivered and he took her hand. "Want to talk about it?"

"I feel terrible, to be honest. I didn't like Linda. I didn't trust her and I lobbed a pretty serious accusation at her and her boyfriend, and now she's dead."

He chose his words carefully. "It's still not clear what her involvement is…was."

"Regardless…" She grimaced. "She shouldn't have been killed, murdered, especially in Orson's house. They loved one another in the beginning and it was their home, once upon a time." She breathed rapidly, struggling for control. "I'm going to have to tell him when he's better."

He sandwiched her cold fingers between his palms. "I'll be there, if you need me."

She sniffed. "Thank you. And…" Her cheeks went rosy. "If your offer to stay in Roman's trailer is still open, I would humbly accept."

He felt the relief course through him like a refreshing breeze. "That would be fine." Fine, or more like phenomenal. She'd be safe, and she'd be close. He didn't fully understand his joy at that last part, why he craved her presence, but it was becoming hard to deny. And having her talking to him again, part of his day-to-day, felt like winning a medal.

Hagerty spoke to them once more, briefly, one at a time.

Kara returned with Pinky, pleased to be told that Catherine would be staying. "I'll let Chase know. I'm going over to the hospital to switch with him now."

"How's Mom?"

"Almost strong enough to forbid us from staying the night."

"Good progress."

"The best." She hugged Garrett and kissed him on the cheek. "Love you, Gare Bear."

Kara was always quick to share her feelings, the truest example of a person with a heart on their sleeve. He squeezed her close. "Love you too, sis. Thanks for the sandwiches." Fifteen minutes later, Hagerty finally allowed them to head back to the ranch.

Garrett made sure to lock the security gate since he knew Chase and Kara had the code. A token effort.

Would Stone have any reason to try and get to Catherine?

It would be a surefire way to force Antonia to come to him, wouldn't it? Unless he already had her, of course. There was no way to know the current whereabouts of either player.

But now there was another murder.

He felt a dark foreboding that things were coming to a head.

With the increased police attention, it would be a matter of time until Stone was recaptured. What would happen when the dragnet closed in?

The situation would explode.

He could almost hear the crackling of the fuse as it burned down to the dynamite.

FIFTEEN

Catherine woke, bleary-eyed and cotton-mouthed. She'd checked her phone obsessively throughout the night, desperate for a message from Antonia in reply to her text.

Uncle Orson's had a heart attack. Stable. CALL ME.

Her phone remained stubbornly silent. Was no news what she should wish for? As much as she was frantic to hear from Antonia, her phone might ring with a bad report from the hospital. She'd followed each pulse-pounding nighttime awakening with a heartfelt prayer that God would spare Antonia and Orson. Now it was morning with no word about either.

The memory of Linda falling, bleeding, dying in the hallway of her uncle's house, intruded. Murder. Now she'd been witness to another life cut short and it reawakened all the trauma of finding her father.

Deep down, she wondered if that was what fueled her sister's wild campaign to deliver justice herself. As if it could somehow sponge away that awful memory.

But vengeance isn't justice, Tony. Killing Stone isn't going to heal anything inside you. How come Antonia didn't realize that? Perhaps she really was stuck in that sixteen-year-old self, forever caught in her own personal horror.

Guilt slithered into her already rattling nerves. Catherine was the big sister and she should have realized Antonia was suffering much more than she'd let on for the last decade. She dialed the hospital and was told her uncle was stable, still heavily sedated. The doctor would call with a report after rounds. She dressed and Pinkerton watched her pad aimlessly around the trailer.

"I know. We could go to the house, where there's coffee and breakfast," she suggested to Pinkerton. *And Garrett.* She'd insisted she was fine with only Pinkerton for a companion so he'd stayed in the house.

Where did they stand exactly? Her anger at him had been misplaced at the hospital and she was sorry for it, relieved to offer an apology. It was embarrassing to admit how much she thought about him, how it had hurt her so deeply to imagine he'd been in favor of harassing her uncle. She knew Garrett Wolfe, and yet she'd set that aside when she'd flown off the handle. Had the decade living as a fugitive damaged her ability to trust? Or was it the violent death of her father? Or both? Maybe it wasn't just Antonia who hadn't healed.

God had brought Garrett into her life when she wasn't ready, wasn't open, hadn't a thought of trusting another human being.

And yet she was trusting him.

And maybe even loving him?

Tidying the minuscule kitchen did not shoo away the strange ponderings. When there was nothing left to tidy, she looked at Pinky, who was still waiting for some sort of decision. "All right. Breakfast it is."

Pinky did not need coaxing. He beetled off the sofa, and out the door, making it to the big front porch without breaking stride. She caught up, knuckles raised to knock, when Garrett opened the door. His smile lit a warm flame inside her.

"Good morning." He handed her a cup of coffee and she realized he'd been watching from the kitchen window, waiting for her to appear.

She blushed and accepted the mug.

"Get any sleep?" he asked.

"No."

"About the same for me."

She splashed some coffee and relinquished her cup to get a paper towel.

"You don't have to do that." Garrett reached for the roll at the same time she did. She stepped to the side, overbalanced and tottered. He took her upper arm to steady her, and suddenly she was drawn close to his chest. A force held them together, as if they were joined by magnets.

He smoothed her hair, his gaze roving her face, like he was trying to memorize every curve. Her breath caught, and she stilled as he cupped the back of her neck with his palm and kissed her. An unattached, shadowy piece of her heart settled into place as his lips met hers. He released her with a look of wonderment and she thought she'd never seen such sweetness in any man's smile. She almost giggled, her senses buzzing. What on earth should she say after that?

"Uh, hope that wasn't too forward of me. I, um, kinda lose my head when you're around."

"I…feel the same." She smiled, unable to figure out how to reply, grateful when a buzz from Garrett's phone caught his attention.

He pulled it from his pocket and frowned. "Unknown number."

Stephanie and Chase arrived then, laptops tucked under their arms, in the middle of a quiet argument. She was relieved they hadn't been witness to the kiss.

Garrett answered the call and his eyes flew wide. The

bottom fell out of Catherine's stomach, draining away the pleasure she'd felt a moment before. Bad news. It was bad news. No, no, no. She gripped the kitchen counter.

Stephanie and Chase hurried over as Garrett activated the speaker and put the phone on the table.

She heard labored breathing, a man's grunt, static.

Garrett leaned closer to the phone. "Stone?"

"I didn't know who else to call."

Catherine clapped her palm across her mouth to contain her scream. Porter Stone was on the line. Had he gotten to her sister? Was he calling to taunt them?

"You did the right thing," Garrett said smoothly. "I can help you. Officer Hagerty—"

"Is champing at the bit to arrest me. Don't shine me on, Garrett. I'm not stupid."

"No, no, of course you're not. You wouldn't have survived this long if you weren't smart." He glanced at his siblings, then his gaze lingered on Catherine. "Let's talk then, Porter. Me and you. Man to man."

"Not on the phone. I need you to hear something."

To hear something? Catherine's hands shook.

Garrett remained implacable. "Okay. Where are you? We can meet. Why don't you come here, to Security Hounds? You know where it is, right?"

He snorted. "Oh, sure. I'll just drive right over and the cops will be there waiting to arrest me."

"Somewhere else then."

"I can't trust you." His voice was edged with hysteria. "I can't trust anyone."

"You can."

"How do I know?"

"Listen to me, Porter. What happened with Mr. Hart all those years ago, I know it was an accident. You didn't mean to. Things got heated, out of hand." He waited for some response but nothing came. "And Orson's wife, Linda…"

"What?" he snapped. "What about Linda?"

Garrett's brow rose. "I was going to say it was another accident. You needed money. Linda found you searching Orson's house so you shot her. Again, you never meant to kill anyone, right?"

The silent seconds ticked by. Stephanie and Chase exchanged puzzled glances.

"Porter? Are you still there?" Garrett said.

"I can't do this anymore. I'm at the Wells Ghost Town. I'll surrender, but only to you, Garrett. I'll tell you everything and—and go with you to the cops. Just you."

"We'll do this however you want, but…" The connection ended. Garrett stared at his phone.

Stephanie was already on her cell. "I need to speak to Chief Hagerty personally," she said. "No. I'll hold."

Chase sat in an armchair, poring over a map on his laptop. "Wells is a deserted mining town turned tourist attraction. Half a dozen buildings, public access, but right now it's closed because of road damage from the extreme snow this winter. It's off Highway 270 about two hours from here."

Stephanie huffed out a breath. "Still holding."

Catherine's thoughts tumbled. Stone was going to give himself up. At last, it would be over. She sent a text to her sister, blinking back tears.

It's over. He's going to surrender.

For years she'd yearned for this very moment, and now it was finally coming to pass.

Garrett seemed to have fallen into a stupor, staring out the kitchen window.

She put a hand on his shoulder. "What are you thinking?"

"I'm not sure." He opened his mouth, closed it, took a breath and started talking. "I have this feeling. Deep down. I don't think we've got the whole picture."

She froze, her hand falling away. He could not be implying what she thought he was. Not now. "Garrett," she said carefully. "You're not saying that you believe Stone is innocent."

"Not innocent, not entirely."

Not *entirely*? Her mouth fell open. "But not guilty?"

Chase looked over at her sharp tone.

"Believe me," Garrett said. "I know this is painful to hear and it's painful to say, but there's a piece missing. Why would he call me? If he wanted to punish Antonia, why contact me? Why suddenly give up now? What does he need me to hear?"

"He's desperate. Trapped, looking for a way out that doesn't get him captured or shot."

Garrett let out a long breath. "He was shocked when I brought up Linda. That wasn't faked. And the crime scene… that box at your uncle's. If it had cash in it, how would Linda's assailant know that? It would have had to be someone familiar with the house."

A rush of emotion tightened her throat. "Maybe Stone went to meet Linda, saw her looking at the money and killed her for it."

He shook his head. "If Linda knew there was cash in that box and she wanted it, she'd have emptied it when Orson was first abducted, wouldn't she? And the gun…"

"What about it?" she demanded.

Chase looked as grim at Garrett. "Last we knew, it was Antonia with the gun, not Stone."

She gaped. "You have got to be kidding me. So now you think Tony killed Linda?"

"No, but—" Garrett began.

She pounded a fist on her thigh. "Stop, please. Just stop."

"Catherine, I don't want to hurt you…"

"Then don't." Her voice shook and her muscles felt as if they'd snap at any moment. Stephanie and Chase were drawn in by the rising volume of her voice, but she couldn't control herself any longer. "Don't tell me that all this time you've been hoping to prove my father's killer innocent."

"I'm not trying to prove anything. I want the truth. That's all."

"The truth?" she said, spitting out the words. "We have it. Stone told you. He's going to turn himself in because he's guilty."

"There's something wrong," Garrett repeated. "I wish there wasn't but there is."

"You're right about that." She lobbed the words at him like grenades. "After everything we've been through, you're still the same person you were ten years ago when you didn't believe me and my sister. As a matter of fact, you'd like my uncle and sister to be guilty in some way so you can clear your conscience. We're a bad family and Stone's some misunderstood kid, is that it? Why did I ever think you'd change?"

He flinched but stood his ground. "This isn't about me justifying my decisions or trying to fix my reputation. I absolutely believed your testimony then and I do now, but you weren't there in the kitchen when your father died. You didn't witness what happened. You didn't see Stone kill him."

She felt her world shattering into jagged shards all over again. Garrett wasn't who she'd believed and she couldn't deny it. "I didn't have to see it, Garrett. Stone killed my father, my aunt and he almost killed my uncle. What does he have to do for you to finally believe in his guilt?" Tears trickled down her cheeks. "Kill my sister? Me? If we're dead, will you be convinced?"

"Don't say that."

She rounded on him, hurt and rage and fear all clattering out of her mouth. "This isn't about the truth. You're trying to prove that you were a good cop. That you didn't make a terrible mistake all those years ago. I understand why it's important to you and your ego, but shouldn't my life mean more than you being right?"

"I..."

The tears dripped from her chin but she did not try to wipe them away. "And that's why you've stayed by me, isn't it? Being so nice? Pretending to care? Not because you saw something special, but because you wanted to help yourself."

He straightened, gaze boring into her. "That's not what this is, Catherine."

"That's exactly what this is." Her fury peaked when she said it, uncontainable. End of story. End of a journey that would not bring the healing her family deserved. She'd rolled into town alone and that's how she should have stayed.

"Go do what you need to do. I will too." She slammed out the door and ran to the trailer, ignoring Garrett's plea for her to stop. She didn't, until she got inside, breath heaving.

A few moments later a car pulled up to the ranch house but she didn't care. Nothing would assuage the hurt. She almost didn't hear her phone. On the third ring she snatched it up, trying to keep the tears out of her voice.

"Sis," she answered.

"What do you mean it's over?" Antonia demanded.

She clutched the phone, swiping the tears from her face with her sleeve. "He called Garrett, Tony. He's agreed to give up. They're on their way to arrest him now. It'll be finished soon."

"Where is he?"

"It doesn't matter."

"This is a ruse and he's going to get away again or kill someone else. Where, Catherine? I'm tired of looking for him."

"I'm not going to tell you that so you can go get yourself killed or kill him and land yourself in jail."

"He's going to murder again. Some innocent bystander. Are you going to allow that?"

"No. It's a safe place, closed to the public because of the winter flooding. You'll—"

"Closed to the public?"

She realized she'd said too much. "I…"

"I know. He talked about Wells Ghost Town when we dated. He's there, isn't he?"

"I'm not sure."

"Yes, you are. I can hear the truth in your voice. Figures he'd go there."

"Antonia, don't."

"I had to make a side trip so it'll take me a while to make it there from where I am. You stay away, sis. I'll get him myself."

"No, Tony. Please." The line went dead.

She glanced back at the ranch house. The front door was open, as was the door of the car that had pulled up. Strange. Whatever the Wolfe family was involved in wasn't her business.

Her heart was bruised and ravaged. Garrett believed Stone because he wanted to heal his own guilt, prove that he'd been right, and that need felt like a chasm between them. It ached so deeply, it drowned out the feeling that had grown inside her for Garrett. Once more she was a helpless teen, watching the most important man in her life leave her behind, set a match to her heart.

Antonia was her baby sister and she was about to ruin her own future for the sake of vengeance.

Her teeth ground together. *No. I won't let her throw herself away.*

The police wouldn't be able to change Tony's mind.

And neither would Garrett.

Catherine was the only one who stood a chance.

With pain carving her heart like a knife, she grabbed her jacket and ran.

Pinkerton and Tank were still barking after Tom Rudden's abrupt arrival. Rudden was unsteady on his feet, eyes red-rimmed and his clothes smelling of alcohol.

Chase had easily avoided Rudden's flailing punch and delivered him safely to the sofa, where he now sat crying.

"You let him go," Rudden wailed at Garrett, spittle flying from his mouth. "You had him ten years ago and you let him get away. And now Linda's dead."

"Calm down, Mr. Rudden," Steph said. "Take some deep breaths."

He shook his head, hair flying. "She was the good one. I did the bad things. Not her."

Chase cocked an eyebrow, hands loose at his sides in case he needed to restrain Rudden. "What bad things?"

He rocked back and forth, pounding a fist on his knee. "I acquired those social security numbers for Orson to give his nieces. Other things too, small stuff. He promised he'd never tell anyone or we'd both go to jail. I went to the hospital to be sure he'd keep his word but he wouldn't wake up. Now…" He spread his palms. "I've lost Linda. I've got nothing left."

Steph and Chase exchanged glances.

Rudden's confession hardly registered with Garrett. The social security numbers were immaterial. He was barely able to breathe after what had happened with Catherine.

And that's why you've stayed by me, isn't it? Being so nice? Pretending to care about me? Not because you saw something special, but because you wanted to help yourself.

He tried to pray, but his concentration was flimsy, wafer-thin.

Vaguely he heard Chase on another line with nonemergency PD, explaining that they had a drunk intruder at the ranch.

Stephanie gripped his bicep, a cell still pressed to her ear. Whatever she'd been about to say was interrupted by Kara's arrival.

"What is going on? I just passed Catherine in an Uber and she looked distraught. The door of the trailer is open and her stuff's still there. Where is she going in such a hurry?"

Garrett jerked. She'd left? Without even packing her things? Everything faded to a dull roar. He knew where she'd gone.

Stephanie explained to Kara what had happened. "Chief," she said finally. "Stone's ready to turn himself in." She launched into a rapid-fire report of the facts.

Kara went to Garrett. "Catherine's gone ahead to Wells, hasn't she? To help her sister?"

"Yes," he replied, grabbing his keys. Pinky bolted to his side.

"Do not go," Stephanie said, palm over the phone. "Garrett, do you hear me?"

Chase looked at him from his position next to Rudden. He didn't say a word, but Garrett knew he understood.

Catherine probably hated Garrett.

But his feelings for her had not diminished one iota.

He would not let her get hurt, even if it meant saving her from herself. Without any kind of plan, he ran to his car and sped off, Pinky's tail smacking the back seat like an out-of-control metronome.

What if he arrived too late?

"What if" isn't an option, Garrett.

You'll get there in time.

You have to.

SIXTEEN

Catherine thanked the man for agreeing to take her close to Wells. She'd been hugely relieved there had been a driver in her vicinity. He'd attempted to make conversation, which she deftly avoided until he shrugged and turned up his radio. When they finally reached the locked gates, he stopped, turning to her uncertainly. "Probably not a great idea to go hiking around though, like I said. All by yourself? What if you fall and get hurt or something? Bitten by a snake?"

"Thank you, but I'll be fine. I know the park is closed. I want to take some photos of the area."

His look said he didn't believe her.

She paid him and got out. He rolled down the window and tried one last time. "You're sure? You don't want me to come back in an hour or so? I won't charge you extra."

"No, thank you. I know what I'm doing."

He sighed and drove away.

In fact, she had no idea whatsoever what she was doing as she walked along the chain-link fence that ran parallel to what would probably be a dusty road in a few months. Now it was muddy, with sunken parts glimmering with collected rainwater. Through the fencing she could peer in at the historic site. It was comprised of several small wood buildings, weathered and leaning. Her hurried internet search had informed her the town was allowed to remain in a state of "arrested decay" that attracted visitors when the place was open.

Arrested decay.

The term made her shudder. A place stuck in the past, like she and her sister.

There was a coil of spiky barbs across the top of the fence. Not insurmountable if a person was willing to give up some skin. How had Stone gotten in? If he'd even told the truth in the first place. Or maybe he'd developed cold feet about surrendering to Garrett and left.

Of one thing she was certain—Antonia wouldn't have deviated from her mission. If she thought there was a chance that Stone was in the historic ruin, she'd comb every building until she found him. Catherine continued to walk as quietly as she could along the fence in search of some clue or an idea that might clarify her own mission, which was starting to feel more futile by the moment. There was not a single indication that anyone was hiding inside.

Until...

She stopped at an irregularity in the fence. A closer examination showed where a large cut had been made, and then the section had been bent back into position to conceal the breach. Her pulse jumped. Was this how Stone had made entry? Or her sister? Or both?

She carefully shoved back the wire and climbed through. The day was cloudy, leaving shadows dappling the decrepit buildings. The smell of mold and old wood tickled her nostrils. Only one building appeared to be more up-to-date because of the modern lock on the front—the bookstore and gift shop. The windows were dark, the door secure when she tried it.

A few yards away was another structure. The wooden building had a significant lean, shored up by a stout beam.

It must have been a hotel at some point, back in those dusty gold-mining days. The windows were shuttered, but one slat was dangling crookedly. She was about to try and get a better look inside when she caught a glimpse of a motorcycle, almost invisible, tucked as it was behind a crumbling rock wall at the rear of the hotel.

Stone.

Her heart pounded and the reality of her situation set in.

There was no sign of Antonia.

Catherine was alone with the man who'd killed her father.

Instead of fear, she bubbled with a fury that was almost uncontainable.

Go face him. Tell him what he's done. Hear his justification for ruining your entire family.

But as profound as her anger was, she would not be foolhardy. Tony was Trigger, not her, and she wasn't going to toss away her safety in a careless moment. She'd retreat to a secure spot, call Hagerty and feed him any details she could to ensure Stone would not have the slimmest chance of reneging on his confession. He'd be caught and her sister's mission thwarted. At least she'd beaten Antonia to Wells. She thanked God for that.

She slunk away from the hotel, moving slowly and picking her way along. When she'd crept around the corner of the bookstore, she took out her phone. There were six texts from Garrett, begging, cajoling, demanding that she stay away from Wells and leave the whole thing to the police.

She would do just that, but Garrett was no longer part of her decision-making. The pain swirled afresh as she ignored the texts and pulled up the keypad to dial the police.

Hagerty's voice bellowed into Garrett's ear as he sped up the desolate drive to the ghost town. "I just talked to Catherine. Stone's there in the hotel building. We're five minutes out. What's your twenty?"

"Arriving now. I see the gate. Still securely closed…wait, there's a hole cut in the wire farther down. Going in."

"No, you're not…" Hagerty's voice faded away.

Garrett let Pinky loose and gave him the command to follow silently. The dog slipped into a trot behind Garrett. They slowed only to shove aside the fence where it had been cut and slip inside. Steph and Chase would be a few minutes behind the cops, having delivered Rudden to the police station along with Kara to explain the situation as best she could.

Garrett pulled his weapon and frantically scanned for Catherine. Where was she? He saw only dilapidated buildings being slowly consumed over time by the world around them. He quickly located the hotel. If Catherine was on the property somewhere, she might be hiding. Had they arrived before Antonia or was she here too? If so, was it possible Catherine had connected with her sister, convinced her to abandon her plan for vengeance?

Pinkerton flapped his ears.

Garrett caught a flicker of movement from the door of the hotel. Yes, it had opened a crack, Pinkerton confirmed with a wag of his tail.

"Good dog," he breathed. "Now stay."

The door opened wider and Garrett took aim with his revolver.

Stone peered out.

"I know you're here, Garrett," he yelled. "I saw your car from the upstairs window."

Maybe he could stop this, get ahead of it. He lowered the weapon. "I came, like you asked. Ready to talk."

"Alone?"

"For now, it's me and the dog. You know the cops will be here soon. You're a savvy guy."

"I figured."

There was a ring of defeat in his voice.

"You wanted me to listen to something. What is it?"

Stone hesitated in the doorway; one hand tugged at the dirty neck of his sweatshirt.

"Come on," he urged. "What's so crucial for me to hear?"

Stone held up his phone. "I…"

Pinky jerked, massive ears picking up on the sound.

"What is it?" Stone said.

Garrett peered around as a rental car plowed through the fence with a horrific squeal of metal. He saw through the shreds of flying wire that Antonia was at the wheel.

Bits of gravel and pieces of the No Trespassing sign flew in every direction.

"Away," Garrett yelled to Pinky, who took off just in time to avoid being run down. Garrett dove from the front bumper, tumbling, then scrambled to his feet again. He had to get to Stone. Force him back inside.

But instead Stone pocketed his phone, whirled and ran for his motorcycle.

"Stone," Garrett shouted.

Antonia braked seconds before she crashed into the hotel, then spun the wheel and changed direction.

Garrett threw himself at the driver's side door, his fingertips grazing the handle before she pulled away.

He had to stop her.

With as much speed as he possessed, he sprinted after the car.

Catherine screamed as a car plowed through the metal fence, narrowly avoiding Pinky. When Garrett flung himself at the driver's door she knew it was futile; her sister wouldn't stop. She saw the tight line of Tony's mouth behind the windshield, her jaw clenched, eyes riveted on Stone as he scrambled onto his motorcycle and gunned it. The car might injure Garrett, Tony herself, Stone, any of them. She was the only chance they had to convince her sister.

"Stop," she shouted, springing from her hiding place and waving. "Don't, Tony. Don't do it."

But Tony didn't slow.

Catherine's tension was unbearable. If Tony killed Stone, she'd turn herself into a murderer just like he was. It would be the worst possible outcome, and one her father would have mourned. Not. Going. To. Happen.

Catherine ran, screaming at her sister, arms flailing. She'd lost sight of Garrett, but she prayed he had not been struck by the runaway car.

The engine revved as Tony closed in on the motorcycle. Catherine ran hard, trying to catch up, pull her sister from behind the wheel, anything to slow the execution that was coming.

Stone was on the move now, gripping the handlebars as he fought to escape. He'd made it almost to the gift shop when he yanked a look behind him, swerved and lost control.

The motorcycle skidded. Stone went flying, body twisting as he somersaulted over the handlebars, disappearing over the stone wall.

Catherine stared in horror. The riderless bike deflected off the stone, pinwheeled over and over, a metallic cyclone moving right toward her.

"Catherine," Garrett yelled.

But she had no time to get out of the way. All she could do was brace for impact. When it came, it was as if she was lifted high into the air and slammed back to earth with such force she thought she'd broken in half. Pain, confusion, a cloud of disbelief.

She heard Garrett yell her name again and the far-off barking of a dog.

A car door opened and there was a sound of running feet. Antonia fell to her knees, crying, stroking Catherine's cheek.

"I'm so sorry," she sobbed.

It's okay, Catherine tried to say, but nothing came out.

She saw a glimpse of Garrett, his face white with shock. He kneeled, hands reaching for her.

"Catherine." The way he said it, the brokenness expressed in that one word, told her everything. She heard the love that underscored the pain and realized what it must have cost him to tell her the truth as he knew it. He'd been wrong, but he had integrity. And he was right about God. God wasn't the cosmic vending machine who'd allowed either of them what they'd wanted, but He'd given Garrett a deep sense of right and wrong, and courage, and he'd been honest, though it had hurt them both.

With a great effort, she reached out her fingers and touched his hand, feeling his tears wetting their joined skin as her world slowly faded to black.

Catherine felt tingles of pain as she swam back to consciousness again. She recognized she was still in the same hospital room and remembered hearing at some point that she'd sustained a concussion and a fractured wrist. An IV attached to her arm tugged as she shifted and she sensed another presence in the room.

Antonia stood at her bedside.

Joy suffused Catherine at the sight of her sister there, whole and safe and not guilty of a man's murder. Garrett had come in earlier, explaining that Stone would survive the motorcycle crash. Tony hadn't killed him and Catherine thanked God for it.

Tony held out her hand and they entwined their fingers, Antonia's cold, clammy almost.

"Are you okay, Cath?"

"Banged-up but nothing permanent," she said, blinking back tears. "And you, Speed Racer? That was quite a performance."

Tony didn't smile. Her gaze seemed to be riveted to the blanket. "I'm fine, physically anyway."

Catherine rejoiced. After the shock wore off, they'd pick up the pieces and restart. But her sister's expression was dire. "What's wrong, Tony?"

She let go of Catherine's hand. "Stone's going to recover. Can you believe it?"

"Yes, but he'll be going to jail for a long time, like he should have done. It's all okay now."

"It's not and he won't," she said softly.

Her temples pounded and she tried to concentrate. "Won't what?"

"Go to jail. Or stay there anyway."

"Of course, he will. What are you talking about? Are you worried he'll escape again?"

Tony grimaced. "Why did Garrett have to interfere?"

Her cheeks flamed at her sister's tone. "He was trying to keep you safe and prevent you from killing Stone. The same reason I was there too."

"I wish he hadn't."

Catherine shook her head, ripples of pain ribboning her skull. "It's over, Tony. And you're not going to jail. That's what matters."

Antonia frowned, fingers curled around the bed rail, her demeanor strange and unfamiliar. "It's not over."

"Yes, it is," she insisted. "Why won't you look at me? What's wrong?"

She glanced up at the lights, grimacing as if they hurt her eyes. "Cath, I came to say goodbye. I have to go."

Goodbye? Catherine sat up, braced against a wave of dizziness. "Go where?"

"Somewhere I can vanish again, with a new identity."

Catherine wondered if the head injury had left her damaged. She simply could not understand what her sister was going on about. She took a breath. "We're okay now. Finally. No more living undercover."

She was still staring at the ceiling. "The cops are going to find out."

"Find out what?"

"What I did."

An icy cold crept over Catherine's body. What had her sister done? "Whatever it is, we can work it out."

"You think so?" Her eyes glittered, feverish, intense. "You always thought you could fix anything, make it all better, didn't you? Well, I murdered our father, sis. And Linda too. How're you gonna smooth that one over?"

Catherine went still, frozen in shock at what she'd heard. "What?" she whispered. "You're—you're confused."

"Oh, how I wish that were true." She was tense as a metal rod, a vein jumping in her jaw. "But you're going to have to face the facts, Catherine. I killed Dad."

I killed Dad. Catherine stared, unable to speak for a moment. "You couldn't have." But she heard the timbre, the brittleness in the statement. Whatever was coming next was going to be the truth whether she was ready for it or not. She gripped the blanket.

Antonia began to rock from foot to foot, arms crossed over her chest. "We argued in the kitchen, Dad and me. I wanted money and freedom, and Dad kept tightening the leash with curfews and rules and cutting my allowance, telling me to stay away from boys, refusing me keys to the car. I said some terrible things, and I got so mad I shoved him as hard as I could." She blinked, watching a memory unfold. "It just… happened, as if someone else did it, not me. He fell and hit his head. I couldn't move. I stood there for a very long time until I realized he'd stopped breathing."

"Oh, no, Tony. No." A violent trembling took hold of Catherine. It was inconceivable, this monstrous confession. It was a dream…no, a nightmare. *Wake up, Catherine. Wake up.*

Antonia shook her head. "Sometimes I can't even believe I did it." Her mouth trembled. "But I didn't mean to kill him. I promise, I didn't."

From somewhere deep within, Catherine summoned the will to comfort. "It was an accident…"

"Yeah, but instead of calling for help, I took Dad's wallet, mopped up some of the blood and ordered a pizza from his phone, knowing Porter was working as the delivery guy that night after his tow truck shift. Porter was such a sap, so gaga about me, he raced right over, probably hoping I'd answer the door."

Porter Stone…walking into a situation that would ruin his life too.

"I opened the front door and waited. He pulled up in his pizza delivery truck, realized something was wrong and walked inside, calling out to see if anyone needed help. I ran to my bedroom and climbed out the window, went around to his car, smeared blood on the handle and tossed Dad's wallet in his front seat. Then I snuck back inside. By that time Porter was in the kitchen and you were too, screaming. I ran in. Porter was trying to help Dad, got blood all over his shoes. I lied…said I'd heard Porter threaten Dad over the phone earlier in the week." Her throat convulsed as she swallowed. "I'll never forget the look on your face. You called the police while I shouted at Porter to get out. He did, so flustered he didn't see the blood smear on his truck or notice the wallet, but the police did after I told them I was sure Porter had killed Dad."

Her shivering increased. "You framed Porter Stone for Dad's murder? This—this can't be real."

"It is," Antonia said, voice hard as steel. "I killed our father." Her mouth trembled, voice dropping to a whisper. "And then I ordered pizza and framed Porter Stone for what I'd done."

"But—but you said he stalked you…all those years."

"I made that up. Uncle Orson was sending money and I needed him to continue, so I concocted the stalker story, faked letters and texts. Sent some to Uncle Orson for good measure. Everything was working out fine. I was living well thanks to Uncle Orson. Porter tried to find me a few times, but I knew he wouldn't show himself because he'd be arrested. I got sloppy. He'd located me online a few months back, a stupid social media account I had with my own picture and a fake name. He knew it was me. He finally figured out I'd framed him and intended to force me to confess what I'd done. I… I was dumb, overconfident that he'd been arrested again, and I posted on my social media that I was going home. After he escaped, he probably found some internet café and looked me up. Knew just where to find me. Maybe he's smarter than he looks."

Facts fell into place. Antonia's determination to find Stone on her own. Stone's insistence on having Garrett listen to something. Proof? "So you went after him."

"In the Burney cabin I slipped up again. He got me talking and used his phone to record my confession. It won't be admissible, but it'll be enough for the cops to reopen the investigation. I can't allow that, can I? Have everyone know what really happened that night?"

Catherine's brain felt sluggish, and her words came out flat and hopeless. "Is that why you tried to kill him again in Wells? By running him down?"

"If you and Garrett hadn't gotten in the middle, he'd be dead, and if the cops looked at the recording on his phone, I could say he'd forced a false confession out of me. But now he's going to recover, and he'll start talking and fill in the details, and Garrett Wolfe already believes him anyway."

Garrett had seen the truth. And been courageous enough to tell her. And she'd severed their relationship because of it.

Pain almost stole away her voice. "Why Linda?" she whispered. "Why did she need to die?"

Her eyes sparked. "You know that woman always hated us."

"Tell me why you killed her," Catherine insisted.

"I needed money. I tried to find some when I stole the gun from Orson's house, but I saw a cop drive by and I was scared of getting caught so I bolted. At the Burney cabin I heard Uncle Orson shouting that he kept cash in a box in his study. He was trying to pay off Stone to let him go. With Stone having my taped confession, I needed funds to leave the country if I couldn't get my hands on him. I went back to Uncle Orson's house. I didn't want to be seen so I went in through the French doors. I was searching for the cash when Linda showed up. She saw me." Antonia shrugged. "I shot her with the gun I took from Orson's study earlier. The security cameras were still offline so there was no proof against me."

One terrible lie had set in motion a cascade that swept her sister into a maelstrom of sin. The pain of it was so great she was not sure she could keep breathing. *Oh, Lord. My sister...my sister.*

Antonia shoved her hands into her jacket pockets. "Anyway, I know you're going to tell the cops."

"I..." How could she not?

Antonia turned away. "I don't fault you for it. It's who you are and they're going to find out anyway. You always were the good one."

"No..." Tears choked her. "I love you, Antonia. You're my sister and I know you didn't mean to hurt our father all those years ago. I will always believe that."

Antonia bent over as if Catherine's comment had pierced her heart. "You're wrong, Catherine. I'm bad. Inside."

Catherine reached out a trembling hand. "You did bad things. Terrible things. It's time to stop. Tell the truth, like Dad would have wanted."

Her agony came out in one, thin wail. "I can't do that, sis. I'm not strong enough to go to prison, to face what I did and have everyone else see." She shook her head. "I love you. Goodbye."

Before Catherine could reply, Antonia hurried to the door.

But Garrett Wolfe was on the other side, quietly watching, Pinky sitting next to him.

Antonia stopped, looked up at him. A long moment of silence passed between them before she sagged. "How does it feel hearing you were right?"

Garrett shook his head. "Like the worst five minutes of my life."

She laughed, bitter and hard. "You're something else, Garrett Wolfe."

Catherine watched Antonia walk by Garrett as Hagerty stepped up behind him.

"You are under arrest for the murders of Abe Hart and Linda Johnson, and the attempted murder of Porter Stone."

Catherine could not hear the rest over her own sobs. Garrett hurried close, Pinky heaving his front paws onto the mattress to comfort her.

Garrett touched her so softly she almost didn't feel it. He'd known Antonia was lying and had Hagerty there to make the arrest, but he'd let her have the moment with her sister, the horrendous unmasking, a last goodbye.

It was the most profound gift he could have given her. The whole terrible truth. At last.

The worst five minutes of her life too.

She sobbed.

He stayed and held her hand.

As the world fell to pieces around her.

SEVENTEEN

Garrett, Kara, Chase and Stephanie watched the blood-hounds romp in the fenced area. Beth lounged in a chair on the porch, probably trying to wrap her mind around the conclusion of the Porter Stone case that her children had spent an hour laying out to her.

"Porter Stone was innocent, all these years. That's tragic. What will happen to him now?" Beth asked.

Garrett rubbed his gritty eyes. "He'll face prosecution for abducting Orson and Catherine, and almost killing me at the cliff behind the cabin, but Hagerty will do his best."

"And so will you," Beth said.

Garrett sank onto the patio chair across from her. "I'll advocate for leniency if the judge will take my thoughts into consideration. Porter was a kid when Antonia framed him. He's lost ten years of his life too. Took him a long time to figure out that the woman he loved had sacrificed him to save herself."

Chase whistled. "Cold. If you and Catherine had arrived five minutes later, he'd have died and no one would ever have suspected his innocence."

"Except Gare Bear," Kara said, tossing a ball over the fence. Tank and Wally watched it fly by, but Chloe and

Pinkerton gamely set off in pursuit. "You always knew, didn't you?"

He sighed. "Suspected. Why doesn't that make me feel any better?"

"Because you're thinking about Catherine," Steph said. "Where is she?"

He looked at the empty trailer, which now seemed barren and unwelcoming since she was gone. "Staying at Orson's house since he's rehabbing there, helping plan a service for Linda. She's reached out to Rudden to include him, but he's not interested."

"Rudden's another victim in all this," Kara said, "but he'll have to take the consequences for his part in stealing the IDs for Orson."

Stephanie nodded. "All right. I'm going to chalk this one up as 'case closed' for Security Hounds. Another successful conclusion."

But it didn't feel anywhere close to successful for Garrett. He'd assumed from the lack of replies to his texts and phone calls that Catherine didn't want to speak to him. She required time, or maybe too much had happened between them that they were now permanently torn apart.

"You need a fresh ice pack, Mom," Kara announced.

"Fresher than the one you gave me fifteen minutes ago?"

"Yep." Kara laughed. "Fresher than that one. And Stephanie's going to make you a cup of hot tea."

"Right." Stephanie opened the back slider. "For how long do you slop in the tea bag again?"

Kara giggled and the two disappeared inside. Beth tipped her face to the sunshine. Garrett kissed her and let himself through the gate into the field to give Pinky a rub as a reward for at least attempting to retrieve the ball that Chloe had snagged. He felt his brother behind him.

"You're here to give me a pep talk?" Garrett said.

"No, to invite you to go bowling with me."

"I'm terrible at bowling."

"That's why I invite you. You're easy to trounce."

They both laughed.

Garrett sighed. "I know what else you're here to do, and you don't have to."

"How's that?"

"I love her."

"I assume we're discussing Catherine," he teased.

"And she's had her world ripped apart and I had a hand in that. She has a million reasons to stay away from me."

"Yes," Chase said, "and there are your horrible bowling skills too."

He ignored the joke. "And I'd be a fool to press her, at this point, with how things are."

Chase folded his arms, one eyebrow quirked, waiting.

"And I'm going to do it anyway because I'm not going to live with any more 'what ifs' or 'why didn't I's.' What do you have to say about that, Chase?"

Chase smiled, stepped aside and grandly swept a palm toward the gate. "About time."

Catherine sat on the stones in a lonely spot near Burney Falls, watching the waterfall thundering down, hoping the vibrations would pound away her agony. All the years and the lies and the sorrow. The last decade, her whole life even, she'd failed to see the truth about her sister. Antonia was impulsive, selfish, self-absorbed. While Catherine knew that her sister had loved their father, her own affection had made it impossible to see Tony's other side, the manipulation, the inability to accept the consequences for her actions, the selfishness that had probably always been there.

Uncle Orson had been equally shocked when she spelled it all out for him. "She let everyone think it was Stone. Killed my wife even," he'd said. He seemed smaller then, sitting in his own hospital bed as she relayed Antonia's confession. "I—I think I must have played a part, giving her everything she asked for and not ever trying to rein her in."

She'd pressed his arm. "What Tony did was not your fault, or my father's or mine. She made a choice and she could not accept responsibility for it." And she would go to jail for a very long time. Catherine would do what she could during the trial and stay as connected as possible no matter what the sentence was, but she would never love and accept blindly, ever again.

The mist from the waterfall bathed her face.

She was not totally surprised when Garrett and Pinky appeared around a bend in the trail. Garrett had been trying to contact her in the four days following her sister's arrest. Or was it five? Six? Everything was still murky and unclear. She'd not been able to think how to respond to his messages, though she'd yearned to. What could she say after what Tony had done? How Catherine had taken her side, stubbornly refusing to hear anything contrary to what she'd wanted to believe.

She couldn't quite look at Garrett, her mouth suddenly dry.

Pinky hustled over, inviting himself half onto her lap and slopping her with his tongue.

"Aww, come on, Pinky. Let the woman have some personal space, huh?" Garrett said.

Pinky meandered off to sniff at the bushes. Garrett settled on a rock next to her, sliding a foil-wrapped package from his pocket. "Muffin? Kara made some and she wanted me to be sure I got you to eat one. One of her finest weeds-and-seeds according to Chase."

Smiling, she took it. "Thank her for me. It was so sweet of her, and you. I'm not very hungry, but I'll have it later."

She watched the tumbling ribbons of water. "I, um, I should have replied to your messages, but…"

"It's okay. You don't need to apologize for anything. It's been a roller coaster for you lately."

A roller coaster…or maybe a train wreck. "You were right about Stone," she blurted.

He shrugged. "Wrong and right don't matter much. I'm just sorry. So, so sorry for what's happened."

He reached tentatively for her arm and the connection was so very tender it made her want to cry. "None of it was your fault, no matter what I accused you of."

His fingers kneaded her shoulder. "Don't hang on to that. Please. I'm not."

And he wouldn't. He was that kind of man. She picked at the foil. "I wanted to ask you for some help."

"Anything. Name it."

"Can you…?" Overwhelmed, she stopped and took a breath.

He waited patiently as she tried to collect herself, his hand now tracing comforting circles on her back.

"Can you arrange for me to see him? Porter?"

Garrett's eyes rounded. "Yes. I can do that if it's what you want."

She wasn't quite sure what she'd say yet, but the terrible regret about what Tony had done needed to be expressed and if her sister couldn't do it, Catherine would. "He's okay now, physically? He'll be free?"

"He's still in the hospital and he'll face charges, but Hagerty's working on getting it all straightened out. He's guilty of abducting you and Orson, but your uncle has indicated he would like to ask that Stone be treated with leniency."

She nodded. "I hope I can figure out what to say to him..."

"God will give you the words." He reached for her hand and squeezed. "And I'll be there too, if you want."

She covered his hand with hers. "You'd do that? After everything I said?"

He chuckled. "What, you think I haven't heard worse from women? In high school, I was voted Most Likely to Get Dumped."

She laughed and it felt good.

"See? Sometimes the court jester thing is a bonus."

"Yes, it is." She sighed. "I'm sorry for..."

He scooted around and took a knee in front of her so she had to look at him. "Catherine, you're not going to apologize anymore. You wanted to believe your sister because you love her. There's nothing to be sorry for." He kept his hold on her hand.

Pinky barked at a squirrel chittering from a high branch.

"Pinky's missed you." He paused. "But not as much as I have."

"I've missed you too," she admitted. "It's just... I'm such a mess. Everything is wreck and ruin around me. I don't know what to hold on to."

"Me." He squeezed her hand, his eyes so bright and sincere. "Hold on to God and hold on to me. Together, that's the way to get through this. Not alone."

Together...it sounded perfect.

"I love you," he said in a voice so soft it barely carried over the rushing water.

She stared at him. How could he? After all of it? Tears

brimmed in her eyes and spilled out in hot trails. Before she could answer, he continued.

"I love you for the way you love people. You hold on, and give your best, even if it hurts you. I'm so grateful that you called me out on the joking stuff. You asked me to be myself because you valued me and that helped me value myself." He went hoarse. "What you've endured…it's made you amazing, or maybe you were amazing before."

She almost did not trust her senses. Could it be happening?

"I feel deep in my soul that God made you for me to adore, if you can tolerate a clown as a partner, that is."

Dreaming. That had to be what she was doing. But he kneeled there, with an expression of hope wrapped in love. It was real. He was real.

When she could speak, she cupped his cheek and kissed him. "I love you, Garrett."

His smile was ebullient, dazzling. He stroked her hair and kissed her. Everything came whirling through her soul, a rush of sadness and grief absorbed by something bigger, steadier and lasting.

"But…" she sniffed. "But I don't know what…or how much I can give you right now. With everything…" She gestured helplessly to the invisible mountain of mess that shadowed her and she started to cry.

"It's okay." He held her until her shivering slowed and comfort began to creep in.

"I know you have a boatload of emotions to deal with, and that will continue as Antonia goes to trial."

Antonia. Trial. Court. Again. The mass of it almost crushed her but she felt his strong touch, the press of his lips on her temple. "I don't even know how to do this," she choked out.

"One day at a time and I want to be there for it, to love

you through it, to pray for you in it and when you're ready, if—if you're ever ready, I'll be right here, waiting."

"Waiting for what?"

"For you. For us. For our future."

Another truth settled over the wound delivered by her sister, the truth that in the midst of the mess, a Godly man loved her and she loved him back. "I love you. So much."

And it was as if the pieces of her heart she'd sensed before settled together again, the way they were meant to fit. There would always be a few missing—her father, the sister she'd known and the innocence she'd lost—but she knew God was offering her something precious, lasting, real.

She hugged Garrett and cried, unable to believe that love had come out of the ashes.

Pinkerton ambled over and added his sloppy kiss to their embrace. Then he sat down to watch, waiting for the moment he'd lead them home.

* * * * *

If you enjoyed this story in the
Security Hounds miniseries by Dana Mentink,
be sure to pick up the previous book

Tracking the Truth

Available now from Love Inspired Suspense!

Dear Reader,

Did you enjoy this second installment in the Security Hounds series? I had great fun writing it, especially Pinkerton the bloodhound. He's a fabulous working dog, but he does have the odd foible. Did you know that bloodhounds are also called "sleuth hounds"? They are absolutely relentless trackers but they have a goofy side too. In real life, I have an adopted shelter dog named Junie. She is a little lacking in practical life skills. My husband says she's a comfort dog, but she's only interested in her own comfort. Nonetheless, we adore this scruffy twelve pounds of trouble in a fur coat. I think God gave us dogs in all their wild and wacky forms to provide us a little taste of unconditional love, don't you?

Thank you for reading the book. God bless and I hope you'll come along for the third in the Security Hounds series!

Sincerely,
Dana Mentink